THE
WALL
BETWEEN
US

DAN SMITH

2 PALMER STREET, FROME, SOMERSET BA11 1DS
WWW.CHICKENHOUSEBOOKS.COM

Text © Dan Smith 2023
Illustration © Matthew Land 2023

First published in Great Britain in 2023
Chicken House
2 Palmer Street
Frome, Somerset BA11 1DS
United Kingdom
www.chickenhousebooks.com

Chicken House/Scholastic Ireland, 89E Lagan Road, Dublin Industrial Estate,
Glasnevin, Dublin D11 HP5F, Republic of Ireland

Cover and interior design by Steve Wells
Typeset by Dorchester Typesetting Group Ltd
Printed and bound in Great Britain by CPI Group (UK) Ltd, Croydon, CR0 4YY

FSC
www.fsc.org
MIX
Paper | Supporting
responsible forestry
FSC® C171272

1 3 5 7 9 10 8 6 4 2

British Library Cataloguing in Publication data available.

ISBN 978-1-912626-76-2
eISBN 978-1-915026-24-8

For anyone who ever needed to escape.

Ministry for State Security

File Number 2372: Document I3

Journal written by Anja Schumann.
Recovered from Anja Schumann after her
arrest on 7 October I96I.

This journal belongs to Anja Schumann, aged 12¾.

Do not read!

SUNDAY 13 AUGUST
(EARLY MORNING)

It is exactly seven minutes past two o'clock in the morning but I can't sleep. Not after everything that has just happened. It's official. The whole world has gone CRAZY!

So, I was asleep (of course I was asleep – it's the middle of the night!) when I heard noises. At first it was just part of my dream (dreams are strange), but then there were engines and banging and voices and I thought it must be morning, but it was still dark so that didn't make any sense, so I got up and went to the window and saw soldiers in the street!

I counted:

Fifteen soldiers (in East German uniforms),

Eleven Volkspolizei (East German police),

Four trucks (army),

Two cars (police).

There was a lot of noise. Truck engines, and people talking and shouting. I could hear sirens in the distance, and when I put my face to the window and looked along the street, I could see a tank at the far end, under the street lamp.

A tank!

The soldiers in front of our apartment were rolling a big tangle of barbed wire right down the middle of our street, cutting it in half all the way along! It is exactly forty-six paces from my side of the street to Monika's side (I check every time I go across, which is every day), and the border runs exactly along the middle, twenty-three paces from each side. We joke about crossing the border to see each other every day, but how will we do that if there is barbed wire in the way?!

The police were standing with their backs to our side so they could face the buildings on Monika's side while the soldiers put out the wire. The police were holding rifles and shouting at people (too many to count!) who were coming out of their apartments to see what was going on, but lights were switching on in all the windows and more and more people were coming out on to the street.

People from our side were going out too, but the police and soldiers ignored them because no one from our side could get past the barbed wire anyway.

Mama and Papa came into my room and told me to get away from the window, but I didn't want to because I could see Monika (12¼) across the street, standing at her window, watching what was going on. Aunt Trudi and Uncle Konrad were right beside her, like a mirror of us in my bedroom. Otto was there, too. He's always sneaking over to stay with Monika at night and I know it's because she puts food out for him even though she says she doesn't. Anyway, he's my cat but I don't mind sharing – Monika isn't just my cousin, she's my best friend in the whole world.

So, then everyone in the street started getting angry. Not at first. At first they were just asking questions, but then they started getting louder and shouting at the police. I could hear them right through my window, asking why the soldiers were putting out the barbed wire, but then the police pushed them away. I saw one man get pushed right over on to the pavement, and one woman was screaming so loudly the police dragged her away and put her in a car. It was hard to tell, but I think it was the woman from the apartment next to Monika's. Frau Beck, I think is her name. Anyway, it was really scary. I hope she's all right.

When things calmed down, most people went back inside their apartments and the soldiers moved along the street, taking their trucks and leaving a trail of curly barbed wire behind them. I can still hear them in the distance, and there's more shouting further away.

I'm supposed to be going back to sleep but all I can think about is:

1) How will I see Monika if there's barbed wire right along the middle of the street?
2) How will Otto get back home? (Papa says Otto will be fine. He says cats are cleverer than the devil and that they can find a way through anything.)
3) How will Uncle Konrad get to work?
4) What's going to happen now?

Papa said this is 'An Important Historical Moment', so I'm going to write down as much as I can in my journal so that I remember <u>everything</u>.

Went out on to the street for a better look. Mama and Papa wanted me to stay inside but all the trucks are gone and there are only a few soldiers on the east side (Monika's side), so they said I could go. Anyway, they wanted to look too, so they couldn't exactly stop me, could they?

The barbed wire looks even worse from close up. It's as tall as I am and the spikes are _really_ sharp (I touched one and nearly cut myself!). There were lots of people on both sides looking at the wire and talking about what happened last night. They said the East German soldiers put barbed wire all the way around West Berlin to stop East Berliners from coming here. They said there were crowds all over Berlin, shouting and getting angry.

Frau Weber (from next door) said she'd heard about a woman who tried to get over to our side of the wire last night but got tangled up in it and had to be pulled out and she was all cut and bleeding. Poor woman! It's horrible even to _think_ about being tangled up in all those spikes!

Monika was outside but we couldn't talk because

she was on her side of the wire (east) and I was on mine (west) and there were lots of people shouting to each other. And there were soldiers on her side, stopping people from getting too close. All we could do was wave and smile. It was exciting, but also sad. I wonder how long the wire will be there for? Hopefully not for long. I'm sure someone will tell them to take it down because Mama and Papa said lots of families will be separated like ours – some even worse – and that's not right. Families shouldn't be split up.

Just now, after supper (bread and butter and slices of grilled sausage that were juicy and delicious!) we watched the news on the television and they showed a map of Germany with Berlin all the way over in the East. There was a thick line around West Berlin. The newsreader said the barbed wire goes all the way around West Berlin now, just like the thick line on his map. It looks like we are just a small island on one side of East Germany. It's a bit scary. They said the East German government put up the barrier because all the people there want to come here. Lots of people have already come here which means they don't have enough people in the East to do jobs and things. Instead of making a barbed-wire fence to keep people in, I think they should just make it nicer in East

Germany. If it was really nice, then people would want to stay.

Papa said a secretary at the office has a husband who is in East Berlin for work, so now he's probably stuck and he will have to stay there for ever. Does that mean Monika will never be able to come over to our side?

There is some good news – Otto came back! He must have found a way through the barbed wire. Papa was right when he said cats always find a way through.

P.S. I cut this out of the newspaper. (Papa said I was allowed.)

THE BORDER IS SEALED!

Early in the morning of 13 August, tanks rolled, floodlights blazed and the streets of Berlin were filled with soldiers. East German police strung barricades right across Berlin, separating East from West. Their machine-gunners were given orders to shoot anyone who tried to cross into the western sectors of the city. Families have been divided and friendships have been shattered.

In the early hours of the morning and throughout the day, West Berliners came out in their thousands to wave torches and shout challenges at the East German police. East Berliners also came out in protest, but police drove them back from the barricades using tear gas and smoke bombs. Sub-machine guns were levelled at the crowds, and one West Berliner was bayonetted in the leg after he came too close to the barricade.

Some citizens of East Berlin managed to make a final bid for freedom – there have been reports of women and children dropping from apartment windows into the helping hands of West Berliners, and of youths climbing over the barricades. One East German schoolboy made a dash for freedom. He slipped through the barbed wire and disappeared into the West German crowd that was cheering his bravery.

East Berlin is now guarded by two armoured divisions, 10,000 armed police, and 2,000 armed militia. Reports suggest that East German workers have already begun to fortify the barricade.

I can't believe what's happening. I feel angry and want to shout at someone. It's the summer holiday and I want to play with Monika but all I can do is wave to her through the barbed wire or from my window. We wave every morning and every night. In the afternoon we go on the street and try to talk through the barbed wire, but it's hard and we have to shout all the time. We played catch, throwing a ball over the wire, but a soldier on Monika's side came over and told her to stop. There are always soldiers at the end of the street on Monika's side. Sometimes they walk up and down to check the wire and tell people to get back.

Monika says Uncle Konrad can't work in West Berlin any more. Dieter (aged 14¾) from further down the street said he'd heard that some people from East Berlin can have a pass to come to our side, so I said maybe Uncle Konrad can get one. But Papa told me it's not true, and that the people in charge of East Berlin want to make sure everyone stays there. People from the East who have families here in the West might come over and not want to go back. And Papa works at the British base, so he should know.

He says it has 'caused a stir'.

P.S. I copied this map from the newspaper today. I'm really good at drawing so it looks amazing. I drew it in pencil first, then went over in pen and didn't even smudge it much. Anyway, it makes West Berlin look like a tiny island in the middle of East Germany! I also wrote some things Papa told me about why Berlin is split in two.

- In 1945, after the war, Germany was split into East and West.
- East Germany is controlled by the Soviet Union (Russia).
- West Germany has a French part, a British part and an American part.
- The capital Berlin (where I live) is right in the middle of East Germany and is split into four sectors: the French Sector, the British Sector and the American Sector, which are in West Berlin (where I live), and the Soviet Sector which is in East Berlin (where Monika lives).
- East Germany (Monika!) is called the German Democratic Republic (GDR).
- West Germany (me!) is called the Federal Republic of Germany (FRG).

File Number 2372: Document I4.I

Letter written by Monika Klein, dated
I5 August I96I.
Recovered from Anja Schumann after her
arrest on 7 October I96I.

15 August 1961

Dear Anja,

You probably won't ever see this letter. I can't post it because someone will read it, and I can't give it to you because you're on the other side of the barbed wire and the soldiers are always watching and won't even let us play catch! Anyway, I'm going to write it and pretend I'm talking to you because I'm so confused about everything. I really miss you and I just want things to be normal, but nothing is normal any more. The whole world has turned upside down and I don't know what to do or what to feel. Everyone is scared or angry or excited. They're all shouting or crying.

At Young Pioneers Herr Wolff took us to help the workers putting out more wire. We had to wear gloves and help carry things, like bricks and bags of cement, but there were people on your side getting angry and shouting that it was wrong to make us help. Herr Wolff told us to ignore them and that the barbed wire is to protect us from people in the West because they are 'the class enemy'. Then all the Pioneers started clapping. Even Angela and Harald. I didn't really understand what was going on (I don't think Angela and Harald understood either), and I didn't clap at first, but Herr Wolff stared at me, and I had to join in. Now I'm afraid Herr Wolff thinks I'm not a good Young Pioneer. I know you think Young Pioneers is stupid anyway, and I'm starting to think you might be right. Except sometimes it's really fun, like when we play games in the park and collect for recycling. And I have friends like Angela and Harald.

People in the street are acting strange. On your side of the wire, they shout and get angry. But on my side, they mostly just stand and stare. I even saw a man and a woman just standing there, looking at the wire and crying. They didn't talk or make any noise at all, but I could see tears on their faces and it was horrible because they were there but not there. Like they were empty. But the subway is the worst. Being on the subway is so quiet it's like being trapped in the dark with hundreds and hundreds of empty people. Like ghosts.

I wish I could talk to you about it. I sometimes talk to Mama and Papa, but it's not the same as talking to you. Anyway, we have to be careful in case someone hears us. Papa got really angry about not being allowed to go to work, because it's on your side of the wire, and he started shouting in the kitchen. He said we should have come over to the West when we had the chance. Mama got really scared and told him to keep his voice down because someone might hear. She said there are informants everywhere, working for the police and the Stasi. Sometimes we can hear Herr Fischer talking upstairs, so he must be able to hear us too. And if someone heard Papa, they might tell the police what he said and they'd come and arrest him. Like Herr and Frau Beck from the apartment next door. Did you see that? On the night the barbed wire came, Herr and Frau Beck were arrested. The police took them away in a car and I haven't seen them since. We don't know what has happened to them. Maybe they won't ever come back. Maybe the Stasi put them in prison or did something to hurt them. I don't want that to happen to Papa.

Lots of love, Monika

THURSDAY 17 AUGUST

Everyone is talking about the soldier who jumped over the wire on Tuesday! It was in all the newspapers, and even on the television. He has the same first name as Uncle Konrad, and the same last name as me! He must be so brave. I wish I was brave enough to jump over the wire and see Monika! What a brave soldier! What a hero!

Papa let me cut this out of his newspaper.

17/08/1961

OVER THE WIRE TO FREEDOM

On 15 August, a soldier from the East German army jumped over the barbed wire to freedom.

The soldier, Konrad Schumann, aged nineteen, was on duty with his unit, guarding the barricade at the Bernauer Street sector border.

Eyewitnesses say that the East German soldier was acting nervously, pacing up and down, and occasionally stopping to push down the two-foot barbed-wire barrier he was guarding. Policemen and bystanders on the western side watched the soldier for over an hour before he began making hand signals to them, indicating his intention to escape.

Photographers on the western side of the border pointed their cameras to distract the other soldiers on the east side. Not wanting to be photographed, the other East German soldiers turned their backs, and the escaping trooper took his chance.

Onlookers called out to him saying, 'Come on' as he ran towards the barrier and leapt over the barricade.

'Thank God,' he said. 'Now I'm a free man.' He dropped his sub-machine gun and threw his helmet into the air.

When they realized what had happened, the rest of the soldiers on the East German side of the barricade just stared in astonishment as the trooper was driven away in a police car.

The barrier around West Berlin was erected on the night of 13 August.

FRIDAY 18 AUGUST

Heidi (aged 12 years and 7 days) and her mama came round today. I wanted to talk about **THE WIRE**, but Heidi just wanted to ride on her new bike that she got for her birthday last week. We rode up and down the street but she's still not very good at it. Not as good as Monika and me.

Monika and I made up hand signals so we can send messages to each other from the window when the soldiers at the end of the street aren't looking. Our hand signals are:

1) Hand wave = Hello (obviously!) or goodbye.
2) Thumbs up = I'm all right.
3) Hand on chest then pointing = I miss you (I think).
4) Two hands together beside head = I'm going to bed.
5) Point at eyes then hand circling = See you tomorrow.

It feels like we're spies and I'm going to make up some more signals. Sometimes, after dark, we flash our torches to each other. I think I might try to learn Morse code, then we can actually talk to each other!

That would be SO GOOD!

Otto is always there with Monika in the evening when she waves and I'm glad. I used to get jealous when he went over to her apartment but now I don't really mind. And anyway, when Otto catches a mouse or a bird (yuck!) he always brings it here which means he loves me more than he loves Monika.

SATURDAY 19 AUGUST

So, this is strange. I saw something last night when I tried to say goodnight to Monika. It was getting dark so I flashed my torch to her but she didn't flash back. I kept flashing and flashing but no reply. I don't know why. Maybe her torch is broken. So, I stopped flashing and then I saw something! At first, I thought it was just a shadow on the corner of Gartenstrasse (not the end where the soldiers guard). But then the shadow moved!! Just a bit, but enough to make me look. And then it moved back into the dark by the corner and disappeared. I'm sure it wasn't a soldier because they were still at the other end of the street.

Thoughts I have had:

Was it a ghost? (VERY scary! But also exciting.)

Was it someone trying to get through the wire? (Exciting!)

Is someone watching me? (Scary.)

Is it someone from the STASI? (**<u>VERY SCARY</u>**!)

I can't stop thinking about the Stasi now. Everyone says they're horrible. Papa says they're a kind of 'secret police', but no one really knows who they are, and they spy on people and arrest them and take them away. Heidi says they kill people for fun but I don't think that's true. I will try to find out some more about them.

SUNDAY 20 AUGUST

Today Oma and Opa came here instead of us going to their house like usual on Sunday. They wanted to come here so they could see Monika and Aunt Trudi and Uncle Konrad across the wire. They said Berlin looks ugly with all the barbed wire (I agree), and they said that on their way here they saw workers building a big wall near the subway station! I was sad that Monika couldn't come for lunch and I know Oma and Opa were sad too, so I gave them extra hugs. We tried to talk over the wire, but soldiers told Monika and Aunt and Uncle to go back inside their apartment. Mama made beef stew with potato dumplings (yum!) and cabbage (not so yum!) for lunch. The grown-ups talked about THE WIRE and I wanted to listen but sometimes they whispered, like when they were in the kitchen. I heard Opa tell Mama that they might never see Monika and Aunt Trudi and Uncle Konrad again! I hate THE WIRE. No one should be allowed to just put barbed wire along a street and split people up. Why can't people just be nice to each other instead of being mean and trying to be in charge all the time?

MONDAY 21 AUGUST

This was in the paper today. I had to ask Mama and Papa to explain it properly. It means that police in the East are making some people move out of their apartments if they are close to <u>THE WIRE</u>! I can't believe it. What if they make Monika move? Can they really do that? I hate them.

21/08/1961

BARRICADES ARE EXTENDED

In the continuing separation of Berlin, concrete walls have been built between Potsdam Square and Hindenburg Square in the Soviet Occupied Zone. A wall has also been built between Dorotheenstrasse and Reichstagufer. Barbed wire has been added to the walls. The People's Police have been sealing all exits to the West, and there are reports that the cellar windows of some houses on the western border have been sealed up or nailed shut.

The northern exit of the Bernauer Strasse underground station has also been walled up.

For East Berliners living in apartments situated directly on the border to West Berlin, the first forced evacuations have begun. Families are being forced to pack their belongings into vans and relocate.

All this comes as Britain announces it will send sixteen tanks and eighteen armoured trucks to reinforce the British garrison.

Yesterday also marked the second day of the visit by US vice-president Lyndon B. Johnson, along with six motorized convoys of the US Army, and 1,500 troops. The convoy made a lap around the city and was met with cheering from several hundred thousand people lining the route.

Some have their doubts that East and West Berlin can be permanently separated, but East German authorities are determined to stop the flow of its citizens to the West.

NO!!!!!! Things are getting worse! Today the workers started building a *wall* in front of the barbed wire! <u>A WALL!!</u> Just like they said in the newspaper! Like Oma and Opa saw near the subway. Mama says they are turning Berlin into a giant prison!

Mama and I went out to see what was going on (Papa was at work). Lots of other people were on the street. Mina (aged 11½) and Axel (aged 9¾) from upstairs thought it was very exciting. They were running up and down the street singing 'our side is better than your side' but they *are* very young, so they're still very childish.

There were trucks on the east side of the wall, full of concrete blocks. Workers were taking the blocks off the truck and building a wall. East German soldiers were guarding them and I think I saw some of the workers crying, so I know they don't want to build it.

And they weren't the only ones crying. I saw Fräulein Schmidt (from the apartment above ours) standing on the steps to our building. She was just standing still, not saying anything, with tears rolling down her cheeks. I sometimes hear her playing the violin in her apartment upstairs. She always plays sad tunes and looks sad even though she's very pretty. Anyway, I wanted to ask her why she was crying, but I don't know her and I've never talked to her and there was SO MUCH happening at once it was very confusing.

On our side of the barbed wire (now also a wall!) there were police, and lots of people watching the workers. People were shouting again, but even worse this time. They were REALLY angry. Even the birds were angry! The magpies were going crazy on the roof opposite, squawking and chattering.

(There were five magpies in all.)

Frau Weber (from next door) was yelling at the East German soldiers. Her face went bright red and I thought she was going to have a heart attack. She started shouting at our police next, telling them to do something, to stop the workers. I thought they were going to arrest her for causing a fuss, but some people from our building made her calm down.

People on the east side were shouting and screaming but the soldiers over there were pulling them back.

I could see Monika and Uncle Konrad. Uncle Konrad was shouting with everyone else, and Monika looked really scared (she's not as brave as me). And then one of the soldiers threw something that looked like a Coca-Cola can but it was smoking with gas that made everyone cough. My eyes were streaming with tears and I could hardly breathe or see anything. Mama dragged me up the steps back into our building. We had to sit with wet towels on our faces until our eyes stopped stinging.

When Papa came home he was <u>REALLY ANGRY</u> about the gas. He said the soldiers had no right to treat us like that. He said they were terrible people.

I wish I could talk to Monika about it. It's really hard not being able to tell her things. I tell Monika everything.

When the workers stopped for the day, the wall was four blocks high in some places. It isn't even straight and the cement is all squeezing out like cream on a cake.

I waved to Monika again tonight. She was standing at her window and Otto was with her (getting a big Monika hug) but then I saw THE SHADOW on the corner of the street again. Now I'm sure it's a person not a ghost. Ghosts aren't real – everyone knows that. It was a man and he was wearing a big coat and a hat even though it's a warm night. He was standing in exactly the same place as before, and then he sneaked away, keeping out of the light. But who is it? What is he doing? Is he watching me?

It's so hard to sleep knowing THE SHADOW is out there. I wonder if it <u>really is</u> a Stasi person????

Ministry for State Security

File Number 2372: Document I4.2

Letter written by Monika Klein, dated
22 August I96I.
Recovered from Anja Schumann after her
arrest on 7 October I96I.

22 August 1961

Dear Anja,

I have so much to tell you, and I wish there was a way to give you my letters but there isn't. Anyway, writing things down makes me feel a bit better because it's as if I am talking to you. I'll try to remember everything I want to say, but the days all feel muddled together at the moment.

First of all, I think you're definitely right about Young Pioneers. I'm starting to really hate going there. I'm sure Herr Wolff thinks I'm a traitor because I said the soldier who jumped over the wire might have done it to go and see his friend. Do you know the soldier I mean? Everyone was talking about it, saying he's a traitor. I just said maybe he wanted to see a friend and Herr Wolff got really angry and made me write 'The soldier who jumped the fence is a traitor to the German Democratic Republic' 500 times. It took ages and my hand was aching so much when I finished. Anyway, I hate Herr Wolff now and I'm not a traitor, but I can see why Papa is always telling me to be careful what I say. Just the other day I was telling him I don't like the wire and I <u>especially</u> don't like the wall they've started to build. We were in the entrance to our building when I said it and then Herr Fischer's door creaked and he came on to the stairs and Papa told me to hush because Herr Fischer might be an informant for the Stasi! I wonder if that's really true? Would Herr Fischer tell the Stasi what I said? Some people think there's a Stasi informant in every building, so maybe Papa is right! The Stasi is so scary, and sometimes they arrest people for saying things, and now I'm worried Herr Fischer heard me and might report me.

That's why Papa told me to stop flashing my torch back at you. He came into my room and saw me doing it and told me to stop and made me promise I won't do it again. He said what if Herr Fischer saw me doing it? What if he thought we were spies and reported us? He said what if he and Mama got taken away like Herr and Frau Beck who we haven't seen since the police took them away. So I'm really sad now that I can't flash my torch back at you, but we still have our hand signals.

Anyway, talking of Herr Fischer, I heard noises in his apartment last night. It was really late and I was trying to sleep but I heard someone knock on his door, then there were footsteps and his front door creaked open. His front door always creaks. After that there were voices, but they were quiet and I couldn't hear what they were saying, and a minute later there were loud noises and a big thump like something heavy had fallen over in Herr Fischer's apartment. Then there were footsteps and Herr Fischer's front door opened (I could tell it was his door because of the creak) and someone came downstairs and left the building. I think it was two people and they were walking slowly, as if they were being careful not to make a noise. But what makes it really strange is that I usually see Herr Fischer when I leave in the morning to go to Young Pioneers. But I didn't see him this morning. I don't know what it means, but something isn't right.

I feel like I'm scared all the time.

Lots of love, Monika

23/08/1961

WOMAN FALLS TO HER DEATH

Yesterday morning, a woman died during an attempt to escape East Berlin.

The entrance and windows of her apartment building were being blocked up, so on the morning of 22 August, the day before her fifty-ninth birthday, Ida Siekmann took her last chance to escape. She threw some of her belongings from the third-floor window of her apartment before jumping into a safety sheet held open for her by West Berlin firefighters.

However, Siekmann jumped before the safety sheet was properly open and she was severely injured when she fell to the pavement below.

Ida Siekmann died on the way to Lazarus Hospital.

In a similar attempt on 19 August, forty-seven-year-old Rudolf Urban, along with several other people, used a rope to lower himself from his apartment in the eastern part of Berlin on to the pavement in the West. However, Rudolf Urban fell from the rope and fractured his leg in several places.

The wall is getting higher every day. It is six blocks high in one place! Papa says the wall and the barbed wire is not on our side of the city, so there's nothing anyone here can do about it.

I can't see Monika from the street now so we have to sit halfway up the steps at the front of our buildings to see each other. The whole place smells like concrete and sweaty workmen and nasty soldiers and petrol fumes from the trucks bringing concrete blocks. The noise is awful.

Mama bought me an ice cream to eat on the step but when Monika came back from her Young Pioneers meeting, she saw me and looked angry. I suddenly felt bad eating the ice cream because I couldn't share it with Monika and I know it's not easy for her to get ice cream.

I went to the library today and wrote down some things about the Stasi. (The librarian gave me some funny looks!)

The Stasi

1) Their proper name is MINISTRY FOR STATE SECURITY.

2) Their motto is 'Shield and Sword of the Party'.

3) They are secret police and spies.

4) They arrest people for saying things or writing things they don't like.

5) Sometimes they arrest people who are never seen again!

6) No one really knows who they are.

7) They have spies in the East AND the West.

8) They make people spy on their friends and neighbours. (I would NEVER do that!)

9) Everyone is scared of them.

10) They torture people!

They sound really scary!

Ministry for State Security

File Number 2372: Document I4.3

Letter written by Monika Klein, dated
26 August 1961.
Recovered from Anja Schumann after her
arrest on 7 October 1961.

26 August 1961

Dear Anja,

Something scary happened and I can't stop thinking about it so I have to tell you. Someone came to our apartment the night after all the trouble in our street when the workers started building the wall. It was late and I was in bed and someone knocked on the door but no one ever comes to visit us, not really. Straight away I thought they had come to arrest Papa because he got so angry when the workers were here and the soldiers used the gas. You remember the gas? Of course you remember it! I had it in my eyes and it made them sting so much! Anyway, you probably saw that Papa was one of the people shouting at the soldiers! So, I was sure someone had reported him and now the Stasi had come to arrest him.

Anyway, I got up but Mama told me to go back to bed so I listened at my bedroom door but I couldn't hear much. Just their voices. And when they left, I went to the window, thinking I was going to see them taking Papa away but I saw a man and a woman wearing suits and carrying briefcases. They got into a black car and drove away, and then I went to ask Mama and Papa what was going on. Mama said the people had come to tell Papa he has a new job. He can't work on your side of the wall now, so they have given him a job in East Berlin. And they said that Mama has been working so hard at the hospital they are going to give her a better job. That sounds like good news, doesn't it? I know Papa was getting bored of not having a job, and Mama will get more money. Except, Mama and Papa didn't look like it was good news. You know how grown-ups look when they're not telling the whole truth? When they smile but you can tell it's not real? And they sort of keep looking at each other? Well, that's how they looked. And when Papa came back from his new job today, I could tell he wasn't happy, but I don't know why. I think it must be a bad job.

Everything is getting so scary now. There are soldiers and police everywhere and even tanks on the street. They blocked up the entrance to the church on Bernauer Street and the wall is getting higher. Everyone at Young Pioneers keeps saying I'll have to move because my apartment is too close to the wall, so I told them I hate the wall. I couldn't help it, and I knew I shouldn't have said it, and to make things even worse, Herr Wolff heard me and he already thinks I'm a traitor! Anyway, he told me I need to be a better Young Pioneer and he made me write lines again. I had to write 'The wall is there to protect us from the class enemy' 200 times. When we have to make teams to play games, no one wants me in their team, and even Angela and Harald hardly talk to me. I hate going to meetings now.

I haven't seen Herr Fischer since that night I heard noises in his apartment. Do you think he was arrested? The more I think about it, the more it sounded like a fight, so maybe the police took him. Or, even worse, the Stasi. Maybe he wasn't an informant at all, like Papa thought. Maybe he said something bad and got into trouble! I also haven't seen Herr and Frau Beck since they were arrested. I wonder where they are? Soon there won't be anybody left in our building.

Lots of love, Monika

SATURDAY 26 AUGUST

This was in Papa's newspaper yesterday. It's horrible. Really horrible. I hope Monika is all right. I **<u>WISH WISH WISH</u>** I could see her. Maybe I should stop looking at Papa's newspaper because it only has bad news!

25/08/1961

BRUTALLY MURDERED!

In the almost two weeks since the barricade was first rolled out, many East Berliners have managed to escape to the West. Some have climbed from windows, others have found quiet, unguarded places to cross. And although soldiers patrol the barrier, no one ever imagined the border guards would actually shoot to kill.

But on the afternoon of 24 August, everything changed. A man, identified as Günter Litfin, was brutally shot and killed while trying to swim to freedom.

Litfin was attempting to swim across Humboldthafen Harbour to the opposite shore on the western side of Berlin, when he was seen by border guards patrolling on the railroad bridge. Guards fired several warning shots, but when Litfin refused to stop, the guards opened fire.

Litfin was hit several times and died before he could reach the West Berlin shore.

East German firemen dragged Litfin's body out of the water three hours later, while hundreds of West Berliners looked on in horror.

SUNDAY 27 AUGUST

I told Mama and Papa about <u>THE SHADOW</u> but I didn't see him last night even though I'm sure he's still there. Next time I see him I'll call them.

It's exactly two weeks since they brought the barbed wire. Two weeks since I've been able to talk to Monika. Two weeks since everything turned upside down. I wish we could just go back to the way things were.

I miss Monika SO MUCH.

Mama says this can't go on. She says they'll never be able to keep a whole city divided.

MONDAY 28 AUGUST

The wall gets a little bit higher every day. It is now ten blocks high in one place, but I am going to make myself stop counting because it makes me too sad and angry. I can only see Monika now if we both sit at the top of the steps into our buildings. Soon we'll only be able to see each other from our bedroom windows.

In other parts of Berlin, the wall is even higher!

I took my bike to the park with Heidi in the afternoon (not the same as going with Monika). Heidi is getting better at riding her bike but she's still not as quick as I am even though she thinks she is. She wanted to race, but when I won, she said it was because I cheated which I didn't. She's a bit annoying sometimes. We saw LOADS of people watching THE WALL being built. It's SO LONG! We even saw two tanks on the bridge! We rode along the wall for a while, and it felt like it went on for ever. Some people were going really close and looking over. Everything smelt like cement.

WEDNESDAY 30 AUGUST

A strange thing happened.

It was such a nice day, perfect for catching the subway to the park with Monika for a picnic but I can't do that. Instead, I was sitting on the top step of our building. Mina and Axel wanted me to play catch but I said no. Otto was beside me, lying in a sunspot. I can't see over THE WALL from the steps any more so I just stared at it and I started to cry. I couldn't help it. I was thinking about going to the park with Monika, or to Uncle Joe's, the American diner, and about sleeping at her house, and how she used to come over for supper. But now everything is so <u>wrong</u>. I can hardly even remember what Monika's voice sounds like, and she's my BEST FRIEND!

Then Fräulein Schmidt from upstairs was coming along the street. She walked past me to go upstairs but stopped and came back and sat next to me on the step. I sometimes hear her playing the violin but I've never spoken to her in my whole life. I've never even taken any notice of her because she's so quiet but today I noticed she has hair that's SO black it shines in the sun, and her eyes are two different colours! I've never seen anyone else with eyes like that. She could see that I was crying, but she didn't ask what was wrong or anything, she just said, 'Did you know the wall goes all the way around West Berlin?'

I told her I *did* know that. I said I had made a drawing for my journal and put a red line around West Berlin. I told her it was like they were turning West Berlin into a prison. Except the prisoners are on the outside, so that doesn't even make sense.

Then Fräulein Schmidt said, 'I know something about prisons.'

I don't know what she meant by that. I think she might have been in prison, but I didn't dare ask. Then she asked me my name and she shook hands with me and said I should call her 'Helene'. She is 29¼ years old and she smells really nice, like strawberries, I think.

Then Helene (it feels weird not calling her 'Fräulein Schmidt', especially writing it down!) said she'd seen me and Monika waving and trying to talk to each other. She said she knew I was missing my friend and I said I was scared Monika might have to move away like in the newspaper. I was trying not to cry but Helene said it was all right for me to cry – which made me cry again. It was a really big snotty cry, too, which made me feel silly but she just smiled in a sad way.

So, this is the strange thing . . .

Helene took off her necklace and showed me the most beautiful little compass hanging from it. It is about the size of the tip of my thumb, and it opens up like a locket and has a shiny mirror inside the lid.

Helene (it still feels strange calling her that!) took the compass off the necklace and gave it to me. She said, 'Compasses are like magic because they show you the way home.' And she said, 'It helped me once, and now I want you to have it.' (Not her <u>exact</u> words, but something like that.)

I wanted to take it but didn't want to take it because it seemed like such a special thing to her, and it wouldn't help me anyway because I was already home, but she made me, and then she showed me how a compass works so you know which way is north. You have to turn the compass so the needle is pointing at N (for north). I liked watching the little needle wobble like it's floating. It made me think of the way birds fly when it's windy.

After that, Helene opened the case she had with her and showed me her violin. She said she stopped playing it for a long time, but her twin brother Niko (aged 29¼), who lives in the American Sector, persuaded her to play again and now she's a violin teacher.

Helene is a bit strange, but she's nice. Her eyes are two different colours. Oh, I already said that.

I have put the compass on a necklace and I am wearing it right now.

Things that are strange about today

Why give the compass to me?

What did Helene (aged 29¼) mean when she said it helped her once?

Does it have anything to do with her saying she knows about prisons?

Did Helene escape from prison? If yes, then why was she <u>in</u> prison?!

I read in the news that another man was shot trying to swim to the West yesterday!

THURSDAY 31 AUGUST

Mama saw the compass on my necklace this morning and said I had to give it back. She took me upstairs and knocked on Helene's door. We could hear the violin playing, then it stopped, then Helene opened the door and a delicious smell came out. It was sweet, like baking, and vanilla, and it made my mouth water. Anyway, Mama told her I should never have taken the compass. I was <u>SO</u> embarrassed! I felt like I'd done something really bad, but Helene said it was all right. She said she wanted me to have the compass because I looked sad, then she asked us to come inside for tea and we had butter cake straight out of the oven and it was delicious. Maybe even better than Mama's butter cake . . . but I would NEVER tell her that because Mama's butter cake is delicious too!

FRIDAY 1 SEPTEMBER

I can't even see Monika from my bedroom window now. THE WALL is too high. It's just a giant block of grey between our apartments. All I can see out of my window is THE WALL. I hate it. It makes me angry and sad every time I look out and see it. It makes me want to shout. I want to break it down. It's like we're all prisoners. Papa says we're not prisoners, but I want to see Monika and I can't, so it feels like I am.

Yesterday evening I went out of our apartment and all the way up the stairwell (forty-seven steps from our floor). I went past Helene's door (I could hear a violin playing) to the top of the building where there is a window looking out on the street. That window is higher up than mine, and higher than the wall, so I can look down into Monika's bedroom. And Monika was there! She saw me, and we waved, but she's so far away I could hardly see her face properly. She was hugging Otto and pretending to make him wave at me.

I flashed my torch, but Monika didn't flash hers back. She never does now.

The light in the stairwell is on a timer so it goes off after 182 seconds unless you push the switch back in. When it went dark, I saw someone walking along the street and knew straight away it was THE SHADOW. I could tell by his hat and long coat. He stopped by the alley next to Monika's building and just stood there. It was dark in the stairwell so I don't know if he could see me or not, but it made the hairs stand up on the back of my neck and I got this awful feeling. It made me feel sick to know he was there. Anyway, Mama and Papa had said I should call them next time I saw him, so I sneaked downstairs to get them. We left the light off and Papa came and looked and even he saw THE SHADOW so I'm not making it up. He's real! We watched for a while but then THE SHADOW walked away along the street and disappeared.

Papa says it might be a man from the Stasi. He says they're everywhere in the East. He says they're 'bad news' and that they kill people and torture them and make people spy for them. They make people tell on their friends and neighbours. Even on their family! Imagine that! He says people are scared to tell their friends things in case their friends tell the Stasi. I can't believe friends would really do that. They can't be real friends. I would never tell Monika's secrets to anyone. I would never get her into trouble or put her in danger. Not ever.

I miss Monika SO MUCH. I got a bit upset about it again this morning and Mama and Papa wanted to cheer me up so they took me to Uncle Joe's in the American Sector. We sat in the booth where there is a big picture of Audrey Hepburn. She is a very beautiful actress and Papa said she was in a film called *Roman Holiday* and a film called *Sabrina*. Our waiter was called Stefan (I think) and he talked to Papa in English and said, 'Holy smokes!' a lot because that is what Americans say.

I had a burger and French fries (extra salt) and a Coca-Cola with ice that was delicious. Mama had spaghetti bolognaise (very messy) and Papa had pizza with:

1) Cheese
2) Tomato
3) Mushrooms (yuck)
4) Sausage (yum!)
5) Onions

It's what Papa always has at Uncle Joe's. He let me have a slice, and it was sooooo good, but I took off the disgusting mushrooms. He had a beer but said it wasn't as good as German beer (he always says that!).

I tried to smile the whole time because it was a special treat and I knew it cost a lot for Mama and Papa but I couldn't help thinking about Monika. Food isn't as good in East Berlin and they don't even have proper Coca-Cola, they have Vita-Cola which isn't as nice. We sometimes used to bring Monika to Uncle Joe's for a treat on her birthday (or mine), so that was all I could think about. Monika's favourite thing to have is the pizza with sausage and no mushrooms.

I hope she's all right.

Ministry for State Security

File Number 2372: Document I4.4

Letter written by Monika Klein, dated
2 September I96I.
Recovered from Anja Schumann after her
arrest on 7 October I96I.

2 September 1961

Dear Anja,

Herr Fischer is definitely not coming back. Someone new has moved into his apartment upstairs. Someone who is really pretty and looks like that actress on the poster in Uncle Joe's. I forgot her name. A few days ago, when I came home from Young Pioneers, there were some men bringing boxes out of Herr Fischer's apartment and putting them into a car. Then Papa saw a woman arrive with two suitcases, and when I was looking out of my window another time, I saw her coming into the building carrying a box.

I heard her singing upstairs that night while I was lying in bed (she has a lovely voice) and then I saw her again the next day. She was wearing a red dress and a red scarf and shiny red shoes. She looked very pretty. She has brown hair that is cut short and looks really fashionable.

Anyway, I think she must work close to where I go for Young Pioneers because I saw her on the subway yesterday but I don't think she noticed me. She was wearing a yellow dress this time with the same red scarf as before and was on her own, just staring through the train window. She looked sad, so I think maybe she has a boyfriend who is in the West and she misses him terribly and wants to see him. I also think she must be an artist or a dancer, or maybe a writer, but she has to work in a boring office and she hates it. Or maybe she is an actress, like Audrey Hepburn (I just remembered her name). Imagine that!

I'm sad that I can't see your bedroom window any more, and that I can't come for lunch on Sundays, but I'm trying not to think about it. I'm also trying not to think about what happened to Herr Fischer or to Herr Beck and Frau Beck who disappeared. I have to be really careful what I say, and I am trying to be good at Young Pioneers. I hope you are happy.

Lots of love, Monika

SUNDAY 3 SEPTEMBER

Holy smokes, something awful happened today!

After we got back from Oma and Opa's house, I went up the stairwell (forty-seven steps) to wave to Monika but she wasn't there. Instead, I saw men putting bricks in the windows on the top floor of her building. I couldn't believe it! I ran downstairs to get Mama and Papa, then we went back up and watched the men make their way around the building, bricking up <u>every single window</u>. I was already crying but I cried even more when they went into Monika's apartment and blocked her bedroom window. Now it's just gone. They've done it in all the buildings on that side of THE WALL, all along the street. It's horrible. I went back later just to stare at the blank brick wall of Monika's apartment and I tried really hard not to cry, but I couldn't help it. Helene found me crying in the stairwell and gave me a hug. It was weird but nice and she smelt like strawberries again. Then she asked if I had the compass so I showed her it on my necklace and she went all funny, like she was going to cry. I asked her what was wrong, and she said there are lots of bad people and bad things in the world, but there are good people and good things too.

Then she told me she was in a prison camp in Poland with her twin brother Niko when she was my age (12¾)! AN ACTUAL PRISON CAMP! She said a guard helped them escape and gave her the compass so they could find their way through the forest to a village where there was someone to look after them. She said it took them three days and they had to cross a river and almost drowned but they finally got to the village where an old man and woman helped them. Helene and Niko (both aged 12¾) had to stay inside for a whole year in case anyone saw them! And if anyone came looking, they had to hide under the floorboards. It sounded really scary. She said the compass gave her luck and reminded her of the kindness of the guard and the old man and woman. Then she said:

'But it has done everything it can for me, so I have

given it to you. And when it has helped you, you have to give it to the next person. <u>The compass should always go forwards. Never backwards.</u>' (It wasn't exactly those words, except for the last bit, which I underlined because that bit is exactly what she said.)

I've just been looking out at Monika's window, wishing I could see her, but there are only bricks now. And then I saw him. THE SHADOW. He was there by the alley. Watching. But what is he watching? Me? Something else? I wonder if he's the one who made them block the windows? He's always there.

He's always watching.

MONDAY 4 SEPTEMBER

Today was the first day back at school. I am in a new class but mostly it is the same people. I sit next to Mathilda (aged 12¾) who has had her hair cut short since I last saw her. Heidi said she liked it better when it was longer, but I think it looks really good. I told Mathilda she looks pretty with short hair.

At break time we were talking about THE WALL. Heidi said some people tried to escape by digging a tunnel under it from the basement of an apartment building. Mathilda said people send messages by throwing notes over it in places where it's not too high yet. I wouldn't dare to do that because the soldiers (and THE SHADOW!) are always watching, but it gave me a brilliant idea! I don't know why I didn't think of it before!! I can't wave goodnight to Monika any more because the workers have bricked up her window, but every night when I _used_ to be able to wave to Monika, Otto was with her . . . and every morning he's back with me! Just like this morning! That means Otto knows a way to get over THE WALL! Clever Otto! (Papa said cats are cleverer than the devil.) Well . . . if Otto can get over THE WALL, then he can take a message to Monika! I thought for ages about what message to send, and HOW I could send it, and then I had another brilliant idea (I'm full of brilliant ideas today). The compass! It opens, and there's a small space inside that's perfect for storing a folded-up piece of paper! So, I put Helene's compass on Otto's collar and hid a note inside. I had to make my writing tiny (which isn't hard because everyone says I have tiny writing anyway) and now I just have to wait.

I hope hope <u>HOPE</u> Monika looks inside the compass.

I signed the note 'A' because it's like a secret code name.

TUESDAY 5 SEPTEMBER

It worked! It really worked! Monika read my note and she sent one back. I got it when Otto came home this morning!

Monika has very messy writing and I can hardly read the note, but it doesn't matter, I am going to keep it for ever. This is so brilliant! Otto is our own secret messenger! Otto is brilliant, and so is my idea to send messages. I'm going to give Otto extra hugs from now on. Clever Otto.

Ministry for State Security

File Number 2372: Documents 23.I and 23.2

Transcript of messages between Anja Schumann and Monika Klein. The messages were recovered from Anja Schumann after her arrest on 7 October I96I. Some messages were attached to Anja Schumann's journal, others were found among the letters written by Monika Klein.

4 September 1961:

Anja Schumann

I met the lady from upstairs. The one who plays the violin. She's called Helene and is really nice. She makes delicious butter cake and gave me a special compass because I was crying. I had a really clever idea to put it on Otto's collar and hide a note inside. I really hope you get this. I miss you SO MUCH. I can't even see you now because there's no window. Love A

Monika Klein

I got your message. I saw the little compass as soon as Otto came into my room. Mama and Papa didn't notice, so it's our secret. It's so horrible they blocked the window. My room is dark now and I can't see you. I hate the wall. It's so ugly. There's a new woman living upstairs instead of Herr Fischer (Hannelore says he was arrested!). Her name is Sabine (I don't know how old she is) and she is really pretty. Love M

Ministry for State Security

File Number 2372: Document I4.5

Letter written by Monika Klein, dated
5 September I961.
Recovered from Anja Schumann after her
arrest on 7 October I961.

5 September 1961

Dear Anja,

I couldn't tell you all this in a note because there isn't enough space but I met the woman from upstairs! As I said, her name is Sabine and up close she is even prettier than Audrey Hepburn. She has kind eyes but she also looks a bit sad. Anyway, yesterday evening while I was doing my homework, I heard her front door creak and I suddenly asked Mama if I could go out on to the street for some fresh air. I don't know why I did it. I didn't even think about it. Anyway, I put on my shoes and hurried out to see Sabine coming down the stairs. So then she stopped and smiled at me and came over and said her name is Fräulein Engel but I should call her Sabine because that's what her friends call her. She was going for a walk to get some fresh air because the workers blocked her windows and she doesn't like it. I said I cried when they blocked my window (which I did) and that I don't like the wall. Sabine doesn't like it either, but she told me not to tell anyone otherwise we would get into trouble and she winked, like we have a secret. And the funny thing is that I got your message that exact same day, saying you met someone upstairs in your building! What a coincidence. And what a good idea to send a note. I never thought of it. Clever Otto!

Then I saw Sabine again this afternoon, after a really horrible day at school. My new teacher Frau Berger (who has a loud voice) kept shouting about how good the wall is. Frau Berger shouts a lot. And then Astrid said that workers were knocking down buildings that are too close to the wall. It's true, I've seen apartments all smashed up, and Peter already had to move apartments because they're going to knock his down. Anyway, Astrid and Andrea started saying the workers are going to knock my building down and I got angry. I'm already sick of people saying it at Young Pioneers, and now they're saying it at school. I tried not to get angry, but I couldn't help it, and Frau Berger told me off. At least she didn't give me lines like Herr Wolff, but it was still a really bad day. When I got home, Sabine was in the hallway and she said: 'Are you all right?' and that made me feel worse. It's weird how if you're feeling sad and angry and then someone is nice to you it just makes you want to cry. I told her about the building being knocked down and how I was scared. She was so nice and told me not to worry. She said she thought we would be safe, and our building is safe, otherwise why did they let her move in? And then later this evening, Sabine brought me a cake! A whole cake! She made it herself from her Oma's recipe and it's delicious. Almost as good as one of your mama's cakes!

Lots of love, Monika

P.S. Hannelore said that her mama's friend's neighbour said that Herr Fischer from upstairs was arrested for being a traitor. So that means he isn't an informant or in the Stasi, and the noises I heard in his apartment that night make sense now. Herr Fischer must have put up a fight and they probably had to knock him out to arrest him. I asked Mama and Papa about it but they told me not to talk about things like that. They said I shouldn't believe everything Hannelore tells me, which I don't.

Ministry for State Security

File Number 2372: Document 5.I

Dead drop note left by Captain ████████,
dated 5 September I96I.

Message reads:
CONTACT MADE.

Ministry for State Security

File Number 2372: Documents 23.3 to 23.9.I

Transcript of messages between Anja Schumann and Monika Klein. The messages were recovered from Anja Schumann after her arrest on 7 October I96I. Some messages were attached to Anja Schumann's journal, others were found among the letters written by Monika Klein.

5 September 1961:

<u>Anja Schumann</u>

Holy smokes! My brilliant idea worked. I'm so clever! We can send messages! Everyone talks about the wall all the time. Heidi at school said some people dug a tunnel under it. I wish we could do that. Imagine if we had our own secret tunnel and we could see each other every day! That would be amazing. Or you could come here and never go back. You could live with us and come to my school! Love A

<u>Monika Klein</u>

I don't think a tunnel would be a good idea. Someone might find it and then we would be in BIG

TROUBLE. There are lots of police and soldiers in the streets. Last week there were nine tanks on the bridge. It was very scary. No one here talks about the wall. Papa said we have to keep quiet in case someone hears. Love M

6 September 1961:

<u>Anja Schumann</u>
I think a tunnel would be exciting. But you're right that we would have to be careful. I think someone was watching me from the street. I wonder if it was a spy? Papa thinks it might have been someone from the Stasi! Love A

<u>Monika Klein</u>
Hannelore says that Herr Fischer from upstairs got arrested, so maybe you really <u>did</u> see someone from the Stasi. Maybe they were watching Herr Fischer because he said something bad. Or did something. Sabine from upstairs said we have to be careful because there are 'informants' everywhere. She made a delicious cake and brought some for us.

7 September 1961:

Anja Schumann
Now we both have someone nice living upstairs and they both bake delicious cakes! A girl in my class (Erika, 12½) said East Berliners like the wall. That made me really angry. Heidi said the police in East Berlin made some people move out of their apartments because they are close to the wall! They can't do that! I'm so angry! I wish I could see you. Love A

Monika Klein
It's true. It happened to a boy in my class! His old apartment is right next to the wall so workers bricked up the windows just like ours, but then they made him move so now he is in a different place. They have knocked his old building down! I'm scared they will make us move. I don't want to go. I want everything to be like it was. Love M

8 September 1961:

Anja Schumann
That's awful! How can they do that? It makes me so angry! What if they make you move and I don't know where you have gone?! What if I never see you again? We have to find a way to bring you here. We have to! Love A

Monika Klein
I wish there was a way for me to come across the wall, too. The wall is too high and there's barbed wire everywhere. The checkpoints have soldiers and police and big dogs. If they catch you, you're in SO much trouble. They even shot someone trying to cross. Did you know that? Love M

Case Number 2372: Document I4.6

Letter written by Monika Klein, dated
8 September I96I.
Recovered from Anja Schumann after her
arrest on 7 October I96I.

8 September 1961

Dear Anja,

I'm getting used to writing letters I know you can't read. I thought about getting Otto to deliver one but it's too big to go in the compass and what if it got lost or someone else read it? We have to be <u>SO</u> careful. I had a terrible dream last night that someone found the notes in Otto's compass except instead of just being notes they were letters I wrote saying how much I hate the wall and Herr Wolff and how we were going to have a secret tunnel, so I was arrested and thrown in prison. It was just a dark room with no light at all and there was something scary in there with me but I couldn't see what it was. It felt like a monster or something bad. It was breathing hard, then it started coming for me. It wanted to hurt me and it got really close and when it was right in front of me, I knew it was Herr Fischer. I couldn't see him but I knew it was him and I knew he was all thin and rotten like he was dead. Then I woke up. It was the worst dream ever and I hope I don't have it again.

And now I keep thinking that someone is watching the apartment building. Especially after you said you saw someone. Is someone spying on us? Maybe we should stop sending notes in case we get in trouble. You don't know what it's like here, always thinking people are watching you, and having to be careful what you say. I even heard that some children report their parents or their friends to the Stasi. Can you imagine that?! I would never do anything like that. I would never report my family and friends!

Lots of love, Monika

SATURDAY 9 SEPTEMBER

I haven't written in my journal properly this week because I've been at school and there's <u>SO MUCH</u> homework to do. I have Herr Meyer for Maths, which is easy, but Herr Stein says I need to use some better words in my writing.

All the teachers at school want to talk about THE WALL in lessons. They keep saying how bad it is, and how it must be horrible for the people stuck on the other side of it. Everyone despises (good word, Herr Stein would like it) THE WALL, and just in my class there are three people who can't see their oma and opa, just like Monika can't!

In History, Frau Wagner said we are 'experiencing a historical event' and that people will talk about

THE WALL for years to come and learn a lot from it. Erika (aged 12½) said she thought the people in the East want the wall but Heidi said they don't and that the East German police are making everyone move house or they are putting them in prison! I almost told them about the boy in Monika's class whose building got knocked down, and about Herr Fischer and Herr Beck and Frau Beck who have gone missing from Monika's building, but I can't say anything or they will know about the notes and I have to keep it secret. Anyway, I <u>want</u> to keep it secret because it's just for me and Monika. I wish I could see her. I'm so scared they will make her move and I won't know where she has gone!

Ministry for State Security

File Number 2372: Documents 23.9.2 and
23.9.3

Transcript of messages between Anja Schumann
and Monika Klein. The messages were
recovered from Anja Schumann after her
arrest on 7 October 1961. Some messages were
attached to Anja Schumann's journal, others
were found among the letters written by
Monika Klein.

9 September 1961:

<u>Anja Schumann</u>
I heard about the man who was shot. It was horrible.
Did you know that some people tried to escape by
jumping out of their windows? Today Mama made
gingerbread and the whole apartment smelt like gin-
ger and it made me think of you because it's your
favourite. I wish I could send some to you or, even
better, bring it to you myself! Love A

<u>Monika Klein</u>
I would LOVE some of your mama's gingerbread!
My mouth is watering just thinking about it!
Love M

SUNDAY 10 SEPTEMBER

Today we were at Oma and Opa's and I started wondering about something . . . how does Otto cross THE WALL to Monika's side? When I look out of my bedroom window, all I can see is grey concrete bricks going much higher than Papa (I measured Papa, and he is 181 cm tall and he thinks the wall is at least 450 cm high). There is barbed wire on the top of THE WALL (and broken glass in some places) so how does Otto get over?

Papa said cats always find a way, and he must be right because Otto can still take messages so I know he's getting across somehow, but even cats can't jump that high.

I have decided something.

I am going to follow Otto tomorrow night and find out. But I'll have to be careful and extra _extra_ EXTRA quiet. Mama and Papa can't know, otherwise they will probably destroy me.

Ministry for State Security

File Number 2372: Documents 23.9.4 to 23.9.7

Transcript of messages between Anja Schumann and Monika Klein. The messages were recovered from Anja Schumann after her arrest on 7 October 1961. Some messages were attached to Anja Schumann's journal, others were found among the letters written by Monika Klein.

10 September 1961:

<u>Anja Schumann</u>
I have had another brilliant idea! Maybe there's a way for us to see each other! Why didn't I think of this before? Love A

<u>Monika Klein</u>
A way for us to see each other?! How? Love M

11 September 1961:

<u>Anja Schumann</u>
I'm going to follow Otto and see where he goes at

night. I'm going to find out how he crosses the wall.
Love A

Monika Klein
Be careful! Don't get into trouble! Love M

MONDAY 11 SEPTEMBER

On my way back from school, I saw Helene from upstairs. She asked if the compass had helped so I told her it had – I didn't say how. I didn't tell her about the secret messages because I was too scared that she would tell someone. Anyway, she didn't ask. She just smiled and said 'good'. I haven't even told Mama and Papa about the messages because they would stop me from sending them.

I'm starting to get scared because I have decided that tonight I will go on a secret mission. I will follow Otto. I'll have to keep him in the apartment until after Mama and Papa have gone to bed, then I'll let him out and follow him. I'm like a spy, preparing for a mission! I'll squeeze my thumbs for luck!

I'm SOOOOOO nervous!

I'm back! Holy smokes, that was exhilarating! (That means 'exciting'.) My mission was a success!

I kept Otto in my room for three hours and seventeen minutes after I went to bed. I was waiting for Mama and Papa to go to bed, and it felt like FOR EVER. Otto tried to climb the curtains but I managed to get him to settle down. When I was sure Mama and Papa were asleep, I took my key and sneaked outside like a spy. I really <u>did</u> feel like a spy.

It was a warm night and it felt exciting and nice to be outside. The street was so quiet. Otto thought it was a game. He skulked (another nice word, Herr Stein would be proud of me!) along the edge of the buildings, and my heart was beating so hard! I kept thinking THE SHADOW might be right there on the other side of the wall. Maybe he could even hear me!

I walked 1,015 steps, keeping up with Otto. I thought I lost him a few times, but then saw him again. He went all the way to the end of our street, almost to Lindenstrasse, then came back and went down the stinky alley near our apartment building. He disappeared behind five bins and I waited for him to come out, but he didn't. I started thinking he'd gone to sleep, or disappeared or something, so I pulled out one of the bins and saw a hole in the bricks, low down on the wall. It must be some kind of drain to let rainwater into the sewers and I think it's supposed to have a grate over it, but it's missing and that's where Otto went. Down the drain. And he didn't come back so now I'm thinking there must be a way out on to the other side of the wall. Otto doesn't go OVER THE WALL, he goes UNDER it! Like those people who tried to make a tunnel.

What if I tried going through it? Is that why there's no grate – because someone else has gone through it? The hole looks big enough for a skinny thing like me to fit through, and I think there's some kind of tunnel. It was too dark to see properly, but I think there's a tunnel. But what is it and what is in there?

1) A stinky sewer? (Yuck!)
2) Rats? (Double-yuck!)
3) Ghosts or monsters? (I don't think so, there's no such thing.)
4) Is it safe?
5) Is it a way for Monika to escape?
6) Could it be our own tunnel without having to dig?

There is a lot for me to think about. I wish there was someone I could talk to, but it has to be a secret.

Ministry for State Security

File Number 2372: Document 23.9.8

Transcript of messages between Anja Schumann and Monika Klein. The messages were recovered from Anja Schumann after her arrest on 7 October 1961. Some messages were attached to Anja Schumann's journal, others were found among the letters written by Monika Klein.

12 September 1961:

<u>Anja Schumann</u>
Holy smokes! I think I have found a secret tunnel under the wall! It might be a way for us to see each other so I'm going to try it tonight. I hope Otto gets to you before I do and you read this note. If you do, leave the kitchen window open! So exciting! Love A

TUESDAY 12 SEPTEMBER

I've been thinking about that hole in the wall all day. IS IT A TUNNEL? I asked my teacher Frau Wagner (who knows everything about history) if there are sewers under Berlin, and she said there are. She said some of them are really big and that she wouldn't be surprised if people from the East use them to escape under THE WALL. (Maybe they already do!) Frau Wagner asked if I was planning an escape and I think she was joking but I can't always tell, so I pretended to laugh but just went bright red. Did she know what I was thinking? What if she wasn't joking? What if she knows? What if she's a spy? The Stasi does have spies in the West too, I read it in a book in the library, and now I can't stop thinking about it. But I can't stop thinking about the hole in the wall, either. It might be a way for me to see Monika, and I really miss her. If it is, then I have to try, don't I? I have to find out. So, I have decided I'm going to go on another mission tonight to look at the drain. I will take my torch and shine it down to have a look. If there is a tunnel (I think there is) and it is big enough (I think it is), I'll go inside. I'll go where Otto goes. Through the drain.

I will need:

1) A torch (which I already have).
2) Boots (so I don't get dirty feet).
3) Coat (in case it gets cold).

Ministry for State Security

File Number 2372: Document I4.7

Letter written by Monika Klein, dated I2
September I96I.
Recovered from Anja Schumann after her
arrest on 7 October I96I.

12 September 1961

Dear Anja,

A tunnel? That's too dangerous! I really want to see you but it is <u>too dangerous</u>. I'm scared just thinking about it. And to make things worse, when I came back from school today, Sabine from upstairs was in the hallway and she was petting Otto! Sabine asked whose cat he is and I said he's your cat and then she asked about you and said that I must miss you so much (I do!) and that it's sad that the wall is stopping us from seeing each other, because friends are very important. But then she said, 'Otto has a lovely locket on his collar,' and I almost died right then, because what if there was a message from you in the locket? (Which there was!)

So I quickly grabbed Otto and picked him up and said the locket is stuck and doesn't open. My hands were shaking and I was so scared and I hope Sabine didn't notice. She even said she could try to open the locket for me, but I said no and held Otto tight and said goodbye. Then, when I brought Otto inside and checked the locket, I found a note from you about a secret tunnel and you're going to try coming here! Imagine if Sabine had seen that note! What if she had read it? I know she's my friend, but I don't want her to know about our notes. I especially don't want her to know about a tunnel! We have to be careful. I'm scared and I don't think you should go through any tunnel. It's too dangerous, but I can't tell you not to because you won't get my note in time and anyway, I really want to see you.

I hope Sabine didn't look too closely at the compass. I keep thinking what if she saw the note? Mama and Papa don't want me to talk to Sabine at all. They said I should call her Fräulein Engel and that I have to be careful what I say to her in case she tells someone, like the police. But I'm careful all the time and I'm getting sick and tired of it. I have to be careful at school and I have to be careful at Young Pioneers because I'm sure Herr Wolff is an informant and I think some of the boys and girls might be too. Maybe even Angela and Harald? But Sabine always smiles and she understands me, and I know she's my friend because she made me a cake and we sometimes walk together to the subway. I also know she doesn't like the wall, and she hates that the smelly workers blocked her windows, because she said so. But still. I hope she didn't see your note.

I'm so nervous because I know you are going to try coming here tonight. I can hardly talk to Mama and Papa, and now I'm writing this letter and my hand is shaking so much.

Please be careful.

Lots of love, Monika

P.S. I will leave the window open like you asked.

Ministry for State Security

File Number 2372: Document 5.2

Dead drop note left by Captain ████████,
dated 13 September 1961.

Message reads:
CONTINUING TO MAKE PROGRESS WITH TARGET.
UNEXPECTED DISCOVERY OF POSSIBLE TUNNEL.
LOCATION CURRENTLY UNKNOWN. WILL MONITOR
THE SITUATION.

WEDNESDAY 13 SEPTEMBER

HOLY SMOKES THAT WAS AMAZING!! The mission was a success! I sneaked out last night and it was brilliant! I'm so excited, I am so clever! I think I might explode! But I'm going too fast. I need to slow down and write it properly.

So, I got everything ready, exactly as planned. I had my big coat with my torch in the pocket. I wore boots and old clothes so I wouldn't get my nice ones dirty from going through the tunnel. After Mama and Papa went to bed, I waited fifty-one minutes until I was sure they were asleep, then I sneaked out. I made a few creaks and almost knocked over the little wooden elephant on the table by the door.

NOTE: BE CAREFUL OF THE WOODEN

ELEPHANT NEXT TIME!

So, I went out and skulked all the way to Otto's alley, and the hole was still right there behind the bins. I got down on my hands and knees and shone the torch inside and saw that it was deep, but not too deep, and there was a low tunnel leading under THE WALL in the direction of the other side of the street.

I was really scared at first and I sat there for ages, looking into the hole wondering if I should go. I wanted to go and didn't want to go because I was scared, but then I just did it without thinking. I just crawled in and dropped down!

Then I was in a tunnel, but on a path next to the wall. On the other side was a long drop down to a kind of canal full of brown water (yuck). It was dirty in the tunnel and smelt like bins (that was probably mostly just the bins), and poo (which was horrible!). It went in the direction of Monika's side of the street. Holy smokes! The other side of the street never felt so far and so close at the same time. But there was enough room for me to crouch-walk so I had to try.

It was disgusting. Dark and stinky and scary. I hated being in the tunnel. My heart was beating fast and I started to think that the ceiling was going to cave in and the whole of Berlin was going to squash me dead. Or I would get eaten by giant rats or Stasi spies would get me. I kept thinking about Heidi saying the Stasi eat people, which I'm sure they don't but it was making me SO SCARED and I'm glad I had the torch with me otherwise it would have been even more terrifying (good word) especially with that long drop down, where there were deeper and bigger sewer tunnels. But I made myself keep going right to the other side of the road. RIGHT UNDER THE WALL!

It only took forty-nine steps to reach the other end (it was hard to count when I was crouch-walking) and when I looked up, I saw a hole just like there is on my side of THE WALL. Except there was a grate across it. It was blocked! The gaps in the grate were big enough for Otto to squeeze through, but not me. But then I grabbed it and gave it a rattle, and I could tell it was loose. All I had to do was push it and slide it out of the way, move some bins, and then I climbed out and I was on Monika's side of THE WALL!

I couldn't believe how easy it was!

So I went to the end of the alley and looked about to see if THE SHADOW was around – which he wasn't – then I sneaked along to Monika's building. It was strange being on the other side. It felt darker, and like THE WALL was watching me, and I was suddenly even more scared than before. It was much scarier than being in the dark, smelly tunnel. I even thought about going back but I REALLY wanted to see Monika, so I kept going. I made sure I didn't go in the light from the lamp posts in case the soldiers at the end of the street saw me, then I crept round the back of Monika's building and climbed through her kitchen window, which was open just like I asked in my note.

I was <u>really</u> extra quiet when I sneaked into Monika's bedroom and she almost peed herself when she saw me. She couldn't believe it was me and she was so excited and we whispered and we hugged and she told me everything and I told her everything and it was so good to see her and we said we were like spies and that we could meet up every night using the tunnel as our special route.

We were very careful not to talk for too long, and then I sneaked back out, along the street, down the alley, and came through the tunnel to get home.

SOME OF THE THINGS I TALKED ABOUT WITH MONIKA:

1) Monika really misses me (of course!) and I really miss her and we will be friends FOR EVER especially now that we have a secret tunnel under THE WALL.

2) Aunt Trudi really misses Mama because they are sisters and best friends (like Monika and me).

3) Uncle Konrad is not allowed to work on my side of the wall any more, so he got a new job, which he hates. Uncle Konrad seems sad or angry a lot of the time, and so does Aunt Trudi.

4) Monika thinks Herr Wolff from Young Pioneers might be an informant. He talks all the time about how brilliant things are on their side of THE WALL.

5) We are like spies because we have a secret way of sending messages (Otto and the compass) and because we have a secret tunnel under THE WALL.

6) I told Monika about how Helene was in a prison camp and used the compass to escape, and how you can't give it back because it always has to go forward.

7) Monika misses Oma and Opa a lot.

I could hardly concentrate at school today because I couldn't stop thinking about going through the secret tunnel to see Monika. I miss her so SO MUCH. She is my best friend EVER and I can't wait to see her again. I have decided to go on another mission tonight. I have bought a bottle of Coca-Cola and I'm going to take two slices of the gingerbread Mama made.

THURSDAY 14 SEPTEMBER

I did it again! Mission accomplished! I went through the tunnel to see Monika AGAIN! I think I might be a bit 'claustrophobic' (a big word that means I don't like being in small places) because I felt horrible in the tunnel. My heart was beating SO FAST and I was SO SCARED! I kept thinking that the roof was going to fall in and that I would be trapped in the dark and I wouldn't be able to breathe. But I made it to the far end. Forty-nine steps. Just forty-nine steps. I said it in my head, over and over again. Forty-nine steps. And when I got to the end I climbed out and sneaked round the back of Monika's apartment and through the window and everything was AMAZING! We ate gingerbread and drank the bottle of Coca-Cola (Monika says Vita-Cola is better, but she's wrong). We talked about music and movies (even though they're not allowed to like Elvis

Presley in East Berlin!). I felt like a spy on a secret mission and now I'm home safe.

I said to Monika that she should tell Aunt Trudi and Uncle Konrad about the tunnel so they can come and live with us. I think Monika is scared, though. She asked if the tunnel is big enough for adults and I said I think so. I saw footprints in the tunnel (bigger than my footprints) and the grate was put back in a different way, so someone else could have used it to go under the wall like I did! I think that made Monika scared but she said she would think of a way to tell Aunt and Uncle. She made me promise not to tell Mama and Papa until she's ready, so I promised and I always keep my promises.

I was tired at school today. I almost fell asleep in the History lesson! I think I stayed at Monika's for too long last night. I want to go every night but have decided not to. I don't want to be so tired that Mama and Papa wonder what I'm up to!

SATURDAY 16 SEPTEMBER

Sneaked through the tunnel to see Monika again last

night. It's SO good to see her. I wish she would tell Aunt Trudi and Uncle Konrad about it so they can all come and live here with me, but Monika says she needs to think about it. I don't think she knows how bad things are in the East. Papa says people in West Berlin know more about East Berlin than the East Berliners know! He says it's because the authorities there keep secrets from everyone. I told Monika she should come straight away!

SUNDAY 17 SEPTEMBER

I'm worried about Monika. She was acting strange when I saw her last night, and she kept saying I shouldn't use the tunnel any more, that it's dangerous. She said someone at school heard about some people who were trying to make a tunnel and the police caught them and took them away and no one knows where they have gone. So I said that's <u>exactly</u> why she should tell Aunt Trudi and Uncle Konrad about our secret tunnel – so they can all come through and live here. Monika said it isn't so bad in East Berlin, which I couldn't believe. I told her about all the awful things in the newspaper, and about all the people being shot, but she said they were traitors! It's as if Monika is a different person! Next time I go, I will take my journal and show Monika the things I have cut out of the newspaper. That way she will see how bad things are and she will _**have**_ to come through the tunnel.

File Number 2372: Document I4.8

Letter written by Monika Klein, dated
I7 September I96I.
Recovered from Anja Schumann after her
arrest on 7 October I96I.

17 September 1961

Oh, Anja, I'm so sorry. I want to tell you everything but I can't and I wouldn't blame you for hating me. I'm so scared I don't know what to do. I can't talk to anybody, not even you. I feel so horrible and stupid and I'm the worst person in the world. I don't deserve to be your friend. I don't know how I will even look at you again. I thought Sabine was my friend but I was wrong. I was so, so wrong. Sabine is not my friend. She is an informant. She is a spy. I should have come through the tunnel when you said to. I should have told Mama and Papa and we should have come with you, but now I can't because Sabine knows all about the tunnel and I can't even warn you.

She caught me yesterday morning in the hallway when I was going to Young Pioneers. I didn't even hear her door creak so she must have oiled it. She came downstairs, being all nice like usual, but when we got outside, she suddenly said, 'I saw your friend Anja on Friday night. In the street on our side of the wall.' But how does she even know what you look like? How did she see you? She must have been spying! My heart was beating so fast and my insides were tumbling around like I was going to be sick, but Sabine was just smiling and saying she heard there was a tunnel near our street but didn't know it was actually *in* our street. Then she said she wants to know where the tunnel is so she can use it to escape, but when I said I didn't know (because I didn't want to get into trouble) she started to get angry. She grabbed my arm and pushed me close to the wall and held me really tight so it hurt. I have a bruise on my arm to prove it. And she wasn't smiling any more. Instead, she was staring really hard at me, and talking quietly like the words coming out of her mouth were poison.

She said if I didn't tell her where the tunnel is, bad things would happen. She said Mama and Papa would be taken away and I wouldn't recognize them when they came back, <u>if they even came back at all</u>. She said she could make sure Mama and Papa are taken away or I could be a hero for our country and give her information. She said I can have a special code name if I want, but I don't want a stupid code name, I just want everything to be how it was before they came and built the wall.

And now I hate myself because I told her where the tunnel is. I had to. I'm so sorry, Anja, but I had to tell her. What else could I do? I was so scared. And when I told her, she smiled again like she was a nice person, and rubbed my arm and said: 'You're a good girl, Monika. A hero.' She probably saw you again last night. She probably knew you were here! But I can't tell you that she knows. I can't tell anyone, because Sabine said that if I do, Mama and Papa will get arrested and I'll never see them again. All I can do is try to make you not use the tunnel. Papa told me not to trust her and he was right, and that's why I was acting so strange last night. That's why I told you not to use the tunnel any more. That's why I tried to tell you how dangerous it is, and that things aren't so bad here. But they are because I'm scared and I thought Sabine was my friend but really she is spying on us, and I wish I could tell you. I wish I could give you all my letters and tell you everything but what if Sabine finds out? What if she does something to Mama and Papa? I'm so scared.

Ministry for State Security

File Number 2372: Document 5.3

Dead drop note left by Captain ███████,
dated 17 September 1961.

Message reads:

TARGET HAS BEEN TURNED. LOCATION OF TUNNEL
IS SITUATED IN ALLEY NEAREST TARGET'S
BUILDING. DO NOT CLOSE TUNNEL. OPPORTUNITY
FOR FURTHER ARRESTS AND INTELLIGENCE. WILL
CONTINUE TO MONITOR.

TUESDAY 19 SEPTEMBER
(MONIKA'S APARTMENT)

Oh, no! I went to Monika's again last night, but all the time we were talking, <u>everything</u> was going wrong. I thought everything was so good because we had our secret tunnel and everything, but now I'm stuck here because the stupid police found it. They found the tunnel and THEY WERE RIGHT THERE! The police or Stasi or both were RIGHT THERE when I tried to get home!

I sneaked out of Monika's window as usual, and went back along the street to the alley where the grate was, but halfway there I heard voices and saw four people in the shadows by the alley. I could tell from their shape they were soldiers (I could see the rifles in their hands) and I couldn't go back, in case they saw me, so I pressed right against the wall, in the darkest place I could find. My heart was thumping _so_ hard! I thought they were going to catch me and put me in prison or shoot me or something worse!

Then more people came out of the alley. I counted seven. Three of them were soldiers who were pointing their rifles at the other four. Then there was shouting and someone started running and a gun fired! It was so loud it made me jump and there was a flash, and one of the people fell down. I think he was SHOT! After that, a truck came and the soldiers put the people in the back. They had to carry the one they shot. I've never seen someone shot before, it was so horrible and it makes me feel sick just thinking about it. And then the truck drove right past me! It had to go on the pavement because THE WALL takes up a lot of the road and I made myself as small as I could, and when the headlights pointed at me, I was sure they would see me. I even thought they slowed down, but I must be really good at hiding because they just drove straight past as if I wasn't there.

When the truck was gone, there were still two soldiers standing at the entrance to the alley. Then I saw someone else. THE SHADOW! I couldn't see him clearly but he was there in his hat and long coat, standing in the darkness watching the soldiers, and now I'm sure he works for the Stasi. After a while he walked away in the opposite direction, but the soldiers stayed right there by the alley and I had to come back to Monika's apartment. Uncle Konrad and Aunt Trudi were already awake because they heard the shooting and they saw me climbing in the kitchen window. I had to tell them everything and they're SO angry!! Aunt Trudi kept telling Uncle Konrad not to shout because people might hear. She says everyone is listening. She says we can't trust anyone.

And now I'm here alone in their apartment because they had to go to work this morning and Monika is at school and I can't go outside or near the windows because someone might see me, and I can't go home.

This is how I feel:
1) Scared.
2) A little bit excited. (?)
3) What am I going to do?
4) How can I get home?
5) Maybe I can go through the tunnel tonight?
6) Will the tunnel be blocked?
7) Who else was using the tunnel, and were they trying to escape?

8) Who did the soldiers shoot?
9) Will the soldiers find me and shoot me?
10) Mama and Papa must be so worried – they have no idea where I am.

WEDNESDAY 20 SEPTEMBER
(MONIKA'S APARTMENT)

Aunt Trudi and Uncle Konrad have mostly stopped being angry with me. I think they're just scared now because they don't know what to do. They speak quietly in case someone is listening through the walls and Uncle Konrad says we'll be in a lot of trouble if the authorities (big word for the people in charge) know I'm here. Monika is frightened the Stasi will take us away or even shoot us, because that's what happens to people in East Berlin. She is really scared and I think she's angry with me because she told me I shouldn't use the tunnel, but I did it anyway.

I can't stop thinking about Mama and Papa. They must be so worried about me. They don't know where I am.

To make things even worse, the tunnel is blocked.

Monika goes past the alley on her way to school and she said the alley is empty now and the drain has been bricked up, so there's no way for me to get home. I thought about asking if we could break the bricks so I could go home but I didn't dare. Anyway, THE SHADOW in the hat (who I now know definitely works for the STASI) is probably still watching the street. We'd get caught and taken away like the people I saw being thrown into the truck. Or maybe we'd get shot. I still can't stop thinking about that. I've never seen anything like it. It was so awful I even dreamt about it, except in my dream it was Uncle Konrad who was shot.

I have caused so much trouble and Mama and Papa must be so worried about me. I asked if they would be allowed to just come and get me, but Aunt Trudi says they would need permission to cross the border but it's impossible to get permission (in case someone tries to escape, which is exactly what Mama and Papa told me).

I'll keep trying to think of ways to get home. I wish I could fly, or float across on a balloon. Or I could swim across the river. Except I might drown, and also someone was shot trying to do that so it's not a good idea.

At least Otto is here. I think he's trapped too

because the drain is blocked. When I cuddle him, I put my face in the fur on his neck and he smells like home.

The only good thing is that I get to see Monika when she comes back from school, even if she is angry with me.

Case Number 2372: Document 5.4

Dead drop note left by Captain ███████████,
dated 2I September I96I.

Message reads:
ANJA SCHUMANN IN HIDING IN KLEIN RESIDENCE.
WILL CONTINUE TO MONITOR AND UNSETTLE.

FRIDAY 22 SEPTEMBER
(MONIKA'S APARTMENT)

I am on my own. Monika has gone to school and Aunt Trudi and Uncle Konrad have gone to work. Otto went out of the window and hasn't come back yet. It's scary on my own in the apartment and I have to be <u>SO</u> quiet. I can't even cough in case someone hears me and wonders who is here. They might think I'm a spy from the West, and I don't want to get shot! There are people everywhere, watching and listening. That's what Aunt Trudi says. I told her about THE SHADOW so she said we all have to be extra careful.

It's really quiet in here. I can hear everything. Things I never usually notice. Pigeons outside making coo-coo noises. They coo five times in a row, every time. I can also hear people talking on the street, cars, little creaks, and noises from the apartment. A baby crying. I even thought I could hear a violin playing. Maybe Helene was playing with the window open across the street. Oh, I wish I was at home. It's so close. Just forty-six steps away if THE WALL wasn't there. I can hear someone upstairs, too, moving about in their apartment and sometimes singing. I wonder if it's the woman Monika told me about? Sabine. If I can hear her, maybe she would be able to hear me! I have to be really quiet.

I asked Uncle Konrad if I can just go to the border and say I got lost but he said that wouldn't work because I don't have papers or a passport and maybe the police will think I'm a spy and give me to the Stasi. But I don't think that would happen because I'm just a girl aged 12¾, but I have to listen to what he says. And I had a horrible thought – what if THE SHADOW caught Otto and read the messages about escaping that I put in the compass? What if that's the reason he found the tunnel and caught those people? What if it's my fault that someone got shot? I can't bear the thought of it!

I want to go home. I want to see Mama and Papa. I wish I could just look across at my apartment, but

I can't even do that because the front windows are bricked up.

When Monika got back from school today, she was acting strange. Especially when I told Aunt Trudi and Uncle Konrad about THE SHADOW. She suddenly went completely white and I could see her hands trembling. I think she blames me for everything and she's right. It's my fault and I can tell she doesn't want me to be here. She hardly said anything before going off to do her homework. I asked her what was wrong and she said she was tired from school, but I think she's angry with me. I think there's something Monika isn't telling me.

This is all my fault.

SATURDAY 23 SEPTEMBER (MONIKA'S APARTMENT)

Didn't do anything today. Read *Max and Moritz* because it was the only book I could find. Everyone went out for a walk without me – 'to keep up appearances' Aunt Trudi said. I had to stay here. They were gone for sixty-three minutes. I walked round the apartment ten times before I got bored of it. Each time is ninety-eight paces, so that's 980 paces. There are five chairs, two beds and three tables here. Aunt Trudi likes to put white lace cloths on things and mostly everything else is brown. Even the wallpaper is brown.

I sat at the kitchen table for a long time doing nothing at all, then I thought I heard footsteps outside in the hallway. I tiptoed to the door in my socks so no one would hear and I listened. I thought I could hear breathing and it was scary, but then I stepped on a creaky floorboard and the breathing stopped as if someone was outside holding their breath. Then Otto came and rubbed against my leg and meowed and I didn't hear anything else so I think I imagined it. I've been in here for too long – I haven't been outside in five days!

Monika is still acting strange. She's always grumpy with me like she's annoyed and I think she was glad to go out with her friends from the Young Pioneers so she didn't have to be with me. I asked her what is wrong because I think there is something she isn't telling me, but she said 'nothing'. I don't want her to hate me for causing so much trouble. I told her I am sorry, but she just said, 'I know' and went to do some schoolwork.

I didn't say anything about the footsteps and the breathing outside the door. I think I imagined it and I don't want Uncle Konrad to get even more cross with me. I can tell he is worried.

I sometimes cry myself to sleep but Monika doesn't say anything even though we have to sleep in the same bed.

Ministry for State Security

File Number 2372: Document I4.9

Letter written by Monika Klein, dated
23 September I96I.
Recovered from Anja Schumann after her
arrest on 7 October I96I.

23 September 1961

Oh, Anja, please don't cry. I know you're sorry, but it's not all your fault. You shouldn't have used the tunnel, but everything else is my fault. I'm the one who told Sabine. I'm the one who should never have talked to her. And when you told Mama and Papa about the shadow, it made me realize it could be Sabine! Maybe Sabine was watching us the whole time when we were waving and flashing our torches, and that means she was just making friends with me so she could use me. I've been so stupid. Why did I think she wanted to be friends with someone like me? She was just tricking me so she could use me to find the tunnel, and now people have been arrested and someone was shot and you're stuck here. Aunt Maria and Uncle Walther must be so worried about you, and I know Mama and Papa are scared, but it's not your fault, it's mine.

Going to school is so hard. I can't concentrate and Frau Berger keeps telling me off. She made me miss lunch as a punishment two days in a row and then Sabine is always right there in the hallway when I leave for school, and she is there when I get back, smiling at me as if nothing has happened. She winks and it makes me feel sick. Do you think she knows you are here? Is that why she winks? To show me it's our secret? I hate her. I hate myself, too. I am an informant and I am horrible. I feel even more horrible because when I go out for a walk or something, I'm glad to be away from you. I want to be with you, but I don't want to be with you because I don't know what to say. I even go out to collect recycling with Harald and Angela just so I don't have to be with you. But you're my best friend. How can you ever forgive me for what I have done?

SUNDAY 24 SEPTEMBER
(MONIKA'S APARTMENT)

Aunt Trudi cooked schnitzel for lunch. We had it with tomato sauce and potatoes and vegetables. The schnitzel was burnt and the potatoes were stuck together in a lump. At least it was tomato sauce instead of mushroom sauce though, because mushrooms are disgusting. Aunt Trudi said Mama was always a better cook and I didn't say anything because I didn't want her to feel bad, but she's right. Mama IS a better cook.

We played a card game called Doppelkopf in the afternoon. Monika played, too, but hardly said anything. Even Uncle Konrad noticed and asked her what was wrong. Monika just shrugged and said 'nothing' (like when I ask her) but I know there's something. I tried to get her to tell me but she wouldn't. She just got cross. I don't understand. We're best friends. We're supposed to tell each other everything. Except, I didn't tell about the footsteps and the breathing, did I? I wonder if I should?

Aunt Trudi taught me a card game to play when I'm on my own. You don't need any other players and it's called Die Farbenelf. Aunt Trudi said I would like it because there's counting and adding up in it.

How to play Die Farbenelf
1) Shuffle the pack of fifty-two cards.
2) Deal four rows of four cards face up (sixteen cards in total).
3) Look for two cards of the same suit that add up to eleven and take them out.
4) Fill the gaps with new cards.
5) Jack, King and Queen can only be taken away all at the same time (have to be the same suit).
6) The aim is to get rid of all the cards and use the whole deck until it's gone.

I miss Mama and Papa. They must be so worried about me. Everyone must be looking for me. I wish there was a way to tell them I'm safe. I wish Otto could take a message for me but the tunnel is blocked now. I should never have come through the tunnel.

I think Monika is starting to hate me.

MONDAY 25 SEPTEMBER (MONIKA'S APARTMENT)

Monika is at school again. I wish I could go to school. I will never EVER again say that school is boring. Sitting here in this apartment on my own is boring. It's like being in a boring prison.

It is three minutes past twelve and so far today I have:

1) Read *Max and Moritz*.
2) Played Die Farbenelf fifty-nine times without getting rid of all the cards even once.
3) Sat in this chair <u>FOR EVER</u>!
4) Walked around the apartment (quietly) 153 times.
5) Drank two glasses of

I just heard it again! The footsteps outside! This time

I'm sure I didn't make it up. I tiptoed to the door and heard the breathing. I think there was someone standing right outside the door. I put my ear to it and I had a really horrible feeling there was someone on the other side doing exactly the same thing! As if we were almost touching! So now I'm sitting here in the bedroom, shaking, and I don't dare make a sound. I'm scared to even breathe! I can't let anyone know I'm here. Should I tell Aunt Trudi and Uncle Konrad? They will be so angry with me. Maybe if I just stay really quiet, everything will be all right. No one will know I'm here.

Update: Holy smokes! There's some good news! Uncle Konrad came back from work tonight and said he has a friend at work called Jannick whose brother might be planning to escape across THE WALL and maybe I can go with them! But Uncle is waiting for more details and has to decide if he can trust Jannick. He could be trying to trick Uncle Konrad, so he has to be sure. Anyway, the escape might have something to do with trains. Imagine that! Escape! Uncle Konrad made me promise not to tell Monika about it. He said it is better if she doesn't know or she might accidentally say something at school or at Young Pioneers. It will be SO hard to keep a secret from my best friend.

Update: Monika came back from school in a bad mood again. She was later than usual and said it was because she went collecting rubbish with some of her friends from Young Pioneers. They take the rubbish to a place to be recycled, but I think she just didn't want to come home and see me. I asked her if she was angry with me, but she just shrugged and said, 'No.'

Ministry for State Security

Case Number 2372: Document 5.5

Dead drop note left by Captain ███████,
dated 25 September 1961.

Message reads:
ANJA SCHUMANN REMAINS IN HIDING IN KLEIN
RESIDENCE. STILL NO INTELLIGENCE OF ESCAPE
ATTEMPT. WILL CONTINUE TO MONITOR AND
UNSETTLE.

TUESDAY 26 SEPTEMBER
(MONIKA'S APARTMENT)

Things are getting even scarier. One of the men at Uncle Konrad's work said he thinks someone was in their apartment when they were out at work yesterday. They said things had been moved in their apartment and put back in the wrong place. Even the clocks were set to the wrong time! I wonder if it's something to do with the escape plan Uncle Konrad told me about? He didn't say so, but he must have been thinking it. Aunt Trudi said the Stasi go into people's homes and move things around so people know someone has been in their home or to make people think they are going crazy. That made me think about the footsteps and the breathing outside so I thought I'd better tell Aunt and Uncle about it.

When I told them, they weren't cross like I thought they would be. They were just really quiet and Uncle Konrad went completely white. After a while he said what if someone came in to move things around in this apartment but found me instead! What if I got caught? And he said he's been thinking about THE SHADOW I saw in the hat and now he's scared someone's watching us.

Monika was scared too, but she wouldn't even look at me, and it made me feel really horrible. She's my best friend but I might have ruined it because I have put them all in danger. Monika has hardly said a word to me since she got back from school! AND she was late again because she had a Young Pioneers meeting. I asked what they did at the meeting but she didn't say much. Just that they sang some songs. I'm starting to think she must like her Young Pioneer friends more than she likes me.

Tonight, Uncle is doing something really clever. He has taken all Monika's clothes out of her wardrobe and is putting a hidden door inside to make a secret hiding place at one side! It's only small, but it's such a good idea! Uncle is so clever. Otto is really interested and keeps trying to get into the secret hiding place and Uncle has to keep pushing him out. Now, if someone comes into the apartment when everyone is out, I can go into the wardrobe, open the secret door and hide behind it. The side of the wardrobe is against the wall in the corner so no one will notice, and when all the clothes and coats are in there no one will see the hinges. It's ingenious (good word I heard from Aunt Trudi).

Update: I just tried out the secret hiding place and it is horrible! It's such a good idea, but it made me feel awful being stuck in there in the dark. It was hot and I felt like I couldn't breathe. I didn't tell Uncle because I don't want him to worry. I started to feel dizzy and confused and sick and I had to count in my head to stay calm. It was even worse than being in the tunnel because I could hardly move. I hope I don't have to go in there ever again. Monika is asleep but I can't sleep. I'm shaking just thinking about going in the wardrobe. I keep thinking about Helene saying that she had to hide under floorboards when she was my age. She must have been so scared.

WEDNESDAY 27 SEPTEMBER
(MONIKA'S APARTMENT)

I'm trying to stay quiet. I'm even writing quietly so my pen doesn't scratch on the paper. And I'm breathing quietly. I don't dare walk around the apartment any more in case I make a creak or something. I'm so scared that someone will hear me or come into the apartment and find me. Or that I will have to go in the wardrobe. It's so hard to be quiet all the time and I really want to:

1) Run around.
2) Shout.
3) Cry.
4) Go outside.
5) Cough.
6) See Mama and Papa.

But I can't do anything. At least when everyone is here, I can sneeze if I need to.

Actually, I did cry a bit, but really REALLY quietly.

Played Die Farbenelf 173 times today, and only managed to make all the cards go out once. I've also read *Max and Moritz* twice. Their tricks are naughty, but I don't think they deserve to be ground up into bits and fed to the ducks. Maybe I do, though! I wish I could go back in time and not use the tunnel and not get stuck here. I don't want to read *Max and Moritz* again, and I don't want to play cards, so now there's not much else to do other than stare at the wall.

I had potato soup and bread for lunch but I had to eat it cold because I can't make any noise heating it up. I had to be careful going into the kitchen because there's a creaky floorboard right by the door. There's one by Monika's bedroom, too, and now the living room door has started squeaking (I just found that out and nearly jumped out of my skin!). The soup was disgusting. It was like eating cold sick, and the bread was dry but I made myself eat everything and I will tell Aunt Trudi it was delicious.

Update: Monika came back from school late again. When I asked where she was, she got angry and said she was collecting rubbish with Angela and Harald from Young Pioneers and she showed me two marks she earned for collecting. She <u>really</u> wanted me to see the coins, which is strange. I told her I was sorry about coming through the tunnel and for causing so much trouble. I said I didn't want her to be angry with me and she said she was sorry too. She was even crying a bit, so I gave her a hug and she gave me a hug back. Then Otto came and squeezed between us because he wanted a hug too and it made us laugh. I haven't laughed for AGES! It felt good to talk to Monika again, but I still think she might be hiding something from me, like she has a secret she can't tell anyone. And sometimes she says she's doing homework but I think she's writing something like a journal. I wish she would tell me what's wrong. I'm her best friend and I would definitely keep it secret.

Ministry for State Security

File Number 2372: Document I4.9.I

Letter written by Monika Klein, dated
27 September I96I.
Recovered from Anja Schumann after her
arrest on 7 October I96I.

27 September 1961

Oh, Anja, I don't know what to do. Sabine knows where I go to school! She knows everything! She was waiting for me at the subway station again when I left school today (she is always waiting for me!) and then she followed me on to the train and sat behind me and said I'm her little mouse. She said I'm her 'eyes and ears' and that I'm a hero because I told her about the tunnel and they arrested four traitors. Because of me. I can tell you know something is wrong, but I can hardly even look at you and I get angry that you used the tunnel and got trapped here, but it's not your fault. It's my fault. I should have stopped you and I should not have been Sabine's friend.

When we were on the train, Sabine told me to take my apartment key out of my pocket and give it to her so no one would see. She said if I didn't, something bad would happen to Mama and Papa. It was weird though, because she looked sad when she said it. Then she made me get off the train one stop early and we went to that place where they make new keys. I had to wait outside and when she came back out, she gave me back my key and gave me two marks and told me to say I was collecting with Young Pioneers if anyone asked where I had been. So now she has a key to our apartment and I'm scared she will give it to the Stasi. Remember how Papa said the Stasi sometimes go into people's apartments and move things around and change the clocks to scare them? Well, what if that happens and someone finds you?

Sabine is always there. She waits in the hallway every morning and winks at me as if she is my friend. It makes me feel sick when she does it because it reminds me that I betrayed you and that I am an informant. And everyone keeps asking me what's wrong, but I can't say anything and I'm scared someone will find out what I have done because then Sabine will arrest Mama and Papa and I will never see them again. How could I have been so stupid? Why did I ever think Sabine would really want to be friends with someone like me? I wish I could just disappear.

THURSDAY 28 SEPTEMBER
(MONIKA'S APARTMENT)

I am SO bored. So far today I have:

1) Played Die Farbenelf 192 times before I got the cards to go out.

2) Read *Max and Moritz* twice. Again. (I know it almost by heart now.)

3) Ate one slice of Sülze (disgusting jelly-meat-slice-thing), one dollop of pickled cucumber salad (yuck!), and two cold boiled potatoes for lunch (Aunt Trudi said it was the best she could manage and nothing needed to be cooked).

4) Traced a picture from *Max and Moritz* as a present for Monika.

5) Cried once (quietly).

6) Wished I hadn't come through the tunnel.

Monika liked the picture. It even made her smile. She's still not the same – and is still avoiding looking at me – but she was a bit better today.

FRIDAY 29 SEPTEMBER
(MONIKA'S APARTMENT)

Another boring day. Monika is at school, Uncle Konrad and Aunt Trudi are at work and

Oh, no. No, no, no, no. No. Something awful happened today. I can't even write about it. I'm shaking so much and I can't even think. I'll write it tomorrow. It was a bad day today. Bad, bad, bad, bad.

Ministry for State Security

Case Number 2372: Document 5.6

Dead drop note left by Captain ████████,
dated 29 September 1961.

Message reads:
ENTERED KLEIN RESIDENCE. NO INTELLIGENCE
FOUND. ANJA SCHUMANN STILL IN HIDING AT
RESIDENCE.

SATURDAY 30 SEPTEMBER
(MONIKA'S APARTMENT)

No sleep last night. Couldn't stop thinking about what happened yesterday.

I was in Monika's bedroom writing in my journal when I heard footsteps outside in the hallway. Otto was on my lap and he jumped up and went out to look but I didn't dare go to the door like before, in case I stepped on the creaky floorboard, but then someone knocked on the front door and my heart nearly stopped! I was so scared I didn't know what to do! I sat ever so still and quiet and hoped they would go away, but they knocked again and again. After a while it stopped and it was quiet. I held my breath and counted to fifty-three in my head before the door handle rattled as if someone was trying to open the door, and then I heard the door unlocking!

I knew it wasn't Uncle Konrad or Aunt Trudi or Monika because they were at work or school, but I couldn't move! I was so scared I COULDN'T MOVE! I just sat there at the little table in Monika's bedroom where the window used to be and I couldn't move or breathe or anything. All I could think about was that the Stasi sometimes go into people's apartments, and I knew I had to go into the wardrobe. But I was too scared. It felt as if I was sitting there <u>for ever</u> not doing anything. I could hear the front door unlock and open. Then someone came into the apartment and stood on the creaky floorboard by the front door. I heard Otto meow and that was when I made myself get up. I took my journal and hurried to the wardrobe as quickly and quietly as I could. I don't know if I made any noise or not, in fact I hardly even remember going into the wardrobe, but that's what I did. I went in and hid behind the secret door Uncle Konrad made.

I put my hand over my mouth to stop me making a noise, but my heart sounded so loud in my ears, I was sure the whole of Berlin would know where I was hiding. I felt like I was going to be sick and everything started spinning. I counted in my head to calm myself down, but it was horrible.

And then someone started moving around inside the apartment. I heard them picking things up and putting them down. Otto was meowing and then the floorboards creaked again when they walked into the kitchen.

When they came into Monika's bedroom, I thought I was going to burst or die from fright. It was so awful. I really thought I was going to die. They were creeping about, opening drawers and I knew, I JUST KNEW what was going to happen next. They were going to open the wardrobe and . . . they did! They were right there. So close! They were looking through the clothes and I could hear the coat hangers scraping on the rack and then silly Otto came into the wardrobe. He was purring, then he scratched at the secret door and the person stopped moving coat hangers. I could hear them breathing! They were close enough for me to reach out and touch them if I hadn't been behind the secret door! I almost just gave up. I almost just opened the door and came out, but then I remembered how Helene hid under the floorboards and I knew I had to be brave like her. Anyway, I was even more scared of who was there than of being in the wardrobe, so I held my breath and listened. Then someone tapped on the secret door as if they were testing it. My whole body was cold and numb and I was shaking so much!

Holy smokes, it was SO close!! SO CLOSE!

They stayed in the bedroom for ages. I think they were just standing there on the other side of the secret door. I could hear them breathing. It was so creepy. Then they went back into the living room and I heard the front door shut and the lock click. I was desperate for a wee and couldn't stop shaking but I didn't dare come out until I was sure they were gone. When I came out, I just sat on the floor and cried and hugged Otto. I was cross with him but it wasn't his fault. He is only a cat.

When Aunt Trudi and Uncle Konrad came back from work, I thought they were going to be SO ANGRY with me but they didn't shout. Aunt Trudi just hugged me and cried a bit, which made me cry again. Monika cried too. In fact, she cried loads and loads and she was really shaking which was weird. Anyone would think SHE was the one who had to hide in the wardrobe when someone was sneaking around the house! Uncle Konrad didn't cry. He just went straight into the bedroom to look and see if there was anything that might give away our secret. Was there anything to show I was here? I don't *think* there was. Please don't let there be.

Update: Didn't do much today. Aunt Trudi and Monika went to the park this afternoon to keep up appearances. Uncle Konrad was at work and I was on my own again. I'm so scared in case the person comes back.

Monika is still acting strange. I think she hates me, and I don't blame her.

SUNDAY 1 OCTOBER (MONIKA'S APARTMENT)

Uncle Konrad thinks it was the Stasi sneaking round the apartment, which is really scary. Uncle says he's still waiting for news from his friend Jannick about the escape, but I need to go home as soon as possible, before anyone knows I'm here (if they don't already). I agree. I want to go home right now. I wish I could grow wings and just fly away. All I need to do is get to the other side of the street. It's only forty-six steps when THE WALL isn't there (I should know, I've counted them enough times), but it might as well be forty-six <u>million</u> steps right now.

I heard Uncle tell Aunt Trudi that he keeps thinking people are watching him. He said the woman upstairs who moved in a few weeks ago keeps giving him funny looks as if she knows something. He must be talking about Monika's friend Sabine. I don't think she would be dangerous, not if she is Monika's friend. Uncle said he really hopes I'm quiet when I'm here on my own. But of <u>COURSE</u> I'm quiet! I hardly dare even move!

I told Monika I was scared. What if I made a noise and the woman upstairs (Sabine) heard me? I know she is Monika's friend but I can't let her know I'm here. What if she *already* knows I'm here? I asked Monika if she thinks the woman already knows but she just said, 'How should I know?', and went to do some schoolwork. Weird. She NEVER does schoolwork on Sundays.

I've made such a mess of things. Why didn't I just stay at home? Why did I have to follow Otto?

Last night I dreamt I was stuck under the floorboards and couldn't get out. It was horrible.

I just want to go home. Please please please let me go home.

MONDAY 2 OCTOBER
(MONIKA'S APARTMENT)

I don't dare leave the bedroom. Not even to go and get my lunch from the kitchen. I am too scared of the creaky floorboards. I am going to stay here, right next to the wardrobe and not make a sound. I won't even play cards. I am just going to sit and listen and write down what I hear.

1) Magpies chattering on the roof (I wish I could see them).
2) People talking just outside on the street.
3) Two people arguing.
4) Footsteps in the apartment upstairs.
5) Twelve cars/trucks going past.
6) One dog barking (it might have been Wolfgang,

the big shepherd dog from further up the street
– he barks a lot).

7) A violin playing. DEFINITELY a violin playing.
It was very faint and I could only hear it when
there was no other noise, but I DEFINITELY
heard it. It must be Helene. It made me feel SO
sad and I couldn't help crying.

I can't stop thinking about Sabine from upstairs after
what Uncle Konrad said about her giving him funny
looks. What if she knows I am here? **How** would she
know? Did she hear me? Would she tell someone?
I've been sitting here for ages, not making a sound,
thinking about her and listening. She has been walking around in her apartment. I can hear her footsteps.
I never really took any notice before, but now I hear
her all the time. I wonder why she isn't at work. She
was quiet for a while, then, at exactly eleven minutes
past twelve I heard her walk across her apartment and
her front door opened and closed. It echoed in the
hallway outside. I dared to creep out of the bedroom
to our front door. I know I said I wouldn't, but I
wanted to know what she looks like and I thought
I could look through the keyhole. She was quiet
coming down the stairs to the main hallway –
REALLY quiet – so I looked through the keyhole

and saw her. First, I saw her feet coming downstairs (red shoes with heels), then her legs and her red skirt, then all of her. She looked pretty. Younger than Mama (more like Helene but with short brown hair). Her shoes click-clacked as she came across the hallway towards the main door of the building but then she stopped and crouched down. I thought maybe she was tying her shoelaces but her shoes didn't have laces, so I moved to get a better view through the keyhole and saw that she was stroking Otto. Otto meowed and rubbed against her leg then came over towards our door. When I looked up at the woman again, she was staring right at our door. But not at the door – at the keyhole! As if she could see me or just *knew* I was there. As if she was looking me right in the eye! I got such a scare. I moved away as quickly as I could.

I'm still shaking.

Update: I told Monika about seeing Sabine but she told me not to tell Uncle Konrad and Aunt Trudi because they will get scared. And she said she saw Sabine today after school and she's sure she doesn't know anything about me being here, but I could tell she didn't want to talk about it. Monika is scared Sabine might find out I'm here, but I said that if she's nice she might help us. Monika went all weird when I said that and made me promise not to tell Uncle Konrad and Aunt Trudi, so I promised. And I always keep my promises.

I can hardly sleep at night. I wake up at every little sound.

Ministry for State Security

Case Number 2372: Document I4.9.2

Letter written by Monika Klein, dated
2 October I96I.
Recovered from Anja Schumann after her
arrest on 7 October I96I.

2 October 1961

Sabine was waiting at the subway again and got on the train with me. She sat really close and the smell of her perfume made me feel sick. She said she knows you are in our apartment because she can hear you during the day, which means you are not as quiet as you think you are. Sabine told me she used her key to get into our apartment and that she found the secret door in the wardrobe, and she knew you were hiding there and that Mama and Papa are traitors for letting a spy hide in our apartment. I said you're not a spy and Mama and Papa are not traitors, and I must have got loud because Sabine pinched my arm and told me to hush. Then she said she could get people to come and take you and Mama and Papa away, and that I will have to live in a special school unless I do what she says. She said that people at Papa's work are planning a big escape. She said they're going to help lots of people escape over the wall, and that Papa is one of the 'ringleaders' and he's in really big trouble! Would Papa really do that? The Stasi are going to arrest and question him, but they won't if I get her some information. She said that if I do that, and they catch everyone, they won't arrest Papa and they will let you go home. If I don't help, they will arrest us all. But I don't know anything about an escape, and I don't know how to find out. And could Papa really be planning an escape? It just doesn't sound right.

I can't sleep now. I can hardly eat, and I have nightmares all the time. I'm so scared and I feel so bad that I have to betray everyone. I know you have nightmares too. I can hear you making noises in your sleep.

WEDNESDAY 4 OCTOBER
(MONIKA'S APARTMENT)

Didn't do anything yesterday or today. Nothing. I'm trying to be as quiet as possible.

THURSDAY 5 OCTOBER
(MONIKA'S APARTMENT)

Good news!

I'm going home!! I can't use the tunnel because it's blocked and there are always soldiers on the street, but there is another way! It's got something to do with Uncle Konrad's friend from work called Jannick.

Jannick's brother is a train driver so Uncle Konrad is going to take me to the Bahnhofstrasse train yard at 8 p.m. on Saturday evening, and after that I don't know what. He wouldn't tell me any more than that. Monika doesn't know anything about it. I am bursting to tell her, but Uncle said it's better if she doesn't know, in case she accidentally tells someone at school or at Young Pioneers. I've been really good. I haven't said a word.

Update: Oh. I *did* say something. I couldn't help it. Monika asked me why I was smiling and I said, 'because I'm going home' before I could stop myself. I feel like I've done something really bad because I promised Uncle Konrad I wouldn't tell anyone. But Monika is my best friend and she's been grumpy with me and I want her to like me so I couldn't keep a WHOLE secret from her. So, I only told her a bit. But I don't think it matters. Friends always share secrets. Monika is the best at keeping secrets and she's my best friend, so she won't tell anyone. And all I told her is that I'm going home the day after tomorrow. I didn't tell her anything else.

I can't wait to see Mama and Papa again and I'm

going to give them the biggest hugs and say sorry so many times!! Sorry, sorry, sorry. If this plan works, I promise I will do all my schoolwork from now until eternity, and I will never get angry with Mama for making me eat vegetables. <u>And</u> I promise to help more. With everything. For ever. And I will never sneak out to go down tunnels.

Ministry for State Security

Case Number 2372: Document 5.7

Dead drop note left by Captain ███████,
dated 5 October 1961.

Message reads:
INTELLIGENCE GAINED FROM TARGET. ESCAPE
ATTEMPT CONFIRMED FOR SATURDAY 7 OCTOBER.
STAND BY FOR FURTHER DETAILS.

FRIDAY 6 OCTOBER
(MONIKA'S APARTMENT)

Holy smokes! I got another bad scare today! I need to calm down and then I'll write about it.

There was someone in the apartment again today! I was in the bedroom (I don't dare leave the bedroom during the day now) and being as quiet as possible when I heard footsteps on the stairs outside. Then someone knocked on the door! Just like last time.

I went straight into the secret place in the wardrobe. I didn't even wait to see if someone would come in the front door, but they did. It wasn't as bad this time in the wardrobe. I wonder if I'm getting used to small spaces? I still felt hot and dizzy and sick, but not as much. I counted in my head again to help stay calm. Someone went into the kitchen, opening cupboards and drawers, then into Uncle Konrad and Aunt Trudi's bedroom. Then they came into Monika's bedroom and checked the wardrobe again. They even knocked on the secret door and I nearly dropped dead right there! I was terrified!! I could hear them <u>RIGHT THERE</u>, so close! I was shaking so much I was scared they would hear me. I thought they were going to open the secret door and find me but they didn't. It was too well hidden. They stayed in the bedroom for ages opening and closing drawers, but they can't have found anything to give me away because I don't have any clothes of my own and I keep my boots with Monika's. And I had my journal with me so no one would find it and know I am here.

I stayed in the secret wardrobe for ages. Even after they had gone, I made myself stay there being <u>REALLY</u> quiet for a long time after the front door closed, just in case the person was being clever and waiting for me to come out of my hiding place. It was horrible. I was hot and dizzy and my heart was beating so fast and I felt like I was going to be stuck in there for ever. But getting caught by the Stasi would be worse. That would be worse than anything.

When Uncle Konrad and Aunt Trudi came back from work, I told them what had happened and Monika said it's a good job I'll be leaving soon. She sounded annoyed with me and that made me feel worse. I feel so bad. So terrible. I think Monika hates me. I hope she doesn't hate me. It feels like she does.

I can't wait for tomorrow night. I'm scared about it, but I'm going home.

Tomorrow!

Home!!!

Ministry for State Security

Case Number 2372: Document 5.8

Dead drop note left by Captain ███████,
dated 6 October 1961.

Message reads:
INTELLIGENCE GAINED FROM TARGET. ESCAPE
ATTEMPT CONFIRMED FOR SATURDAY 7 OCTOBER,
8 P.M., BAHNHOFSTRASSE TRAIN YARD.

SATURDAY 7 OCTOBER 1961

<u>5.30 p.m.</u>

Anja, Monika and Aunt Trudi were waiting for Uncle Konrad to return from work. They were all sitting on the sofa in the living room, hardly speaking. Anja had her hands clasped tight between her knees and Monika was biting her fingernails. Aunt Trudi was shaking her leg so much the whole sofa was moving.

Something big was about to happen.

When they heard footsteps in the hallway outside, nobody spoke. They just listened. Anja tried to decide if they were Uncle Konrad's footsteps or if someone else had come into the building. The Stasi, perhaps. Maybe they had discovered that she had been hiding in the apartment and they had finally come to take her away.

The steps approached along the hallway to the apartment door and Anja clenched her fists when she heard the gentle scrape of a key in the lock, followed by the turn of metal on metal as the lock clicked open.

Aunt Trudi stopped shaking her leg.

Monika held her fingers to her mouth.

Please be Uncle, please be Uncle, Anja repeated over and over in her head as the door opened.

Please be Uncle.

Anja didn't dare look. She closed her eyes as the door swung open.

'Konrad!' Aunt Trudi said with relief, and Anja opened her eyes to see her uncle standing in the doorway. His shoulders were wet, as if it were raining outside.

As soon as he closed the door, Aunt Trudi hurried over to hug him. They stood for a while like that, then Uncle Konrad broke away and looked at Anja.

'It's on,' he said. 'Tonight's the night.'

'I'll make schnitzel,' Aunt Trudi said.

Anja didn't think she'd be able to eat even one bite.

Anja had just one mouthful of schnitzel, but it was dry and tasteless and her stomach was churning. She couldn't even face the idea of another bite, so she washed it down with water and left her knife and fork on the plate.

'We're meeting Jannick and his brother in the train yard at eight o'clock,' Uncle Konrad said, looking directly at Monika. 'Anja already knows that.'

Monika said nothing.

Uncle Konrad sipped his glass of water then frowned. 'Jannick's brother is a train driver. He has persuaded his bosses to let him run a train tonight, to improve his skills, and he's going to take it along a disused track that used to cross the border. We are going to be on that train. Some of Jannick's friends and family are meeting at the yard and getting on the train too. The train will leave at exactly eight o'clock, then Jannick's brother will drive the train towards the border. There is a barrier across the track now, but the track is still there, so . . .' Uncle Konrad took a deep breath and looked at each one of them in turn before putting his glass down on the table. 'Jannick's brother is going to crash the train right through the barrier.'

Anja noticed that Uncle Konrad's hands were trembling.

'Is that safe?' Aunt Trudi asked. Her voice was almost a whisper.

'Yes and no,' Uncle Konrad replied. 'Jannick says his brother thinks the train can go through the barrier quite easily, but guards might shoot at us, so—'

'Shoot at us?!' Anja gasped.

'Yes,' said Uncle Konrad. 'Guards might shoot at us. It will be dangerous. We'll be in a carriage right at the front and the train will be travelling quickly, so we should pass the guards before they realize what is happening . . . but we will have to lie on the floor when we get close to the border. To be safe.'

'Wait.' Monika stopped him. 'You keep saying "we"?'

'Yes.' Aunt Trudi leant across the table and put her hand on Monika's. 'You see, we're all going, my darling. We're *all* going across to the West.'

Monika's eyes were filled with fear and surprise. 'But we can't. It's too dangerous. Papa has to help Anja escape and we have to stay here. That's how it *has* to be.'

'No, darling, *this* is how it has to be.' Aunt Trudi squeezed Monika's hand. 'I know you're scared, but this is what we have to do. We—'

'We don't have time for this,' Uncle Konrad interrupted. 'We have to leave soon. But we can't take anything with us. Not a thing. People might be watching.'

'You mean the Stasi?' Anja asked.

'We don't know.' Aunt Trudi shook her head. 'It could be anyone. Anyone at all.'

'What we are doing is very dangerous,' said Uncle Konrad, sounding more serious than Anja had ever heard him. 'If we're caught, we'll be in trouble. A *lot* of trouble. We have to be sure no one takes any notice of us. We have to be sure no one follows us.'

'We shouldn't go,' Monika said, pulling her hand away from Aunt Trudi. 'Not all of us.'

'This isn't up for discussion,' Uncle Konrad told her. 'It's too dangerous for us to stay. I am sure someone knows Anja is here, and that puts us all in danger. We have to leave and it has to be tonight. No argument, do you understand?'

Anja glanced at Monika who was biting her fingernails again.

'Do you understand?' Uncle Konrad repeated.

'We understand,' Anja said.

'Good.' Uncle Konrad took a deep breath and looked at Monika. 'You both have to be very brave and do exactly as I say.'

Anja nodded.

But then she had a sudden thought.

'What about Otto?' she asked. 'I can't leave without him.'

'Where is he?' Uncle asked.

'I don't know; he went out of the window.'

'Then we have to leave him,' Uncle said. 'He'll have to find his own way home.'

'But the drain is covered,' Anja protested. 'There *is* no way home.'

'Then he's stuck here.' Uncle Konrad thumped a fist on the table hard enough to make the cutlery rattle on the plates. He closed his eyes and took a deep breath before opening them again. 'I'm sorry,' he said. 'We just don't have time.'

'I'm sorry, too,' Aunt Trudi said to Anja. 'But we have to leave Otto.'

Anja's throat tightened and warm tears stung her eyes, so she made herself remember what Papa had told her – cats always find a way. The only thing was, Otto hadn't found a way to the other side. He had been here the whole time Anja had.

She couldn't believe she had to leave him behind.

Uncle Konrad stared at the clock on the kitchen shelf for a moment, then wiped his mouth and stood up.

'It's time to go,' he said. 'We can't be late.'

6.45 p.m.
Anja noticed that she wasn't the only one who hadn't eaten the schnitzel.

6.52 p.m.
They left with nothing but their coats and shoes. It was the first time Anja had been out of the apartment in nineteen days, so she was glad to be free from what had started to feel like a prison, but she was also afraid of what could happen in the next few hours. And her heart was heavy for Otto. He was her friend and she was abandoning him. She was also worried about Monika, who hadn't spoken since she had said she didn't want to leave.

With those thoughts, Anja stood silently beside Monika in the main hallway of the building, waiting for Uncle Konrad to lock the front door of the apartment. It was odd that he was locking it, because they were not planning on coming back. None of them would see the apartment again, or anything in it, so what did it matter if it was locked or not?

As Uncle Konrad turned the key, Anja heard footsteps and looked up to see a pair of red shoes coming downstairs from one of the other apartments. Anja recognized the shoes straight away. She had seen them a few days ago, when she had been watching through the keyhole. Anja remembered how the woman who owned the red shoes had petted Otto then looked across as if she had known Anja was watching her.

Anja had guessed who she was. She was Monika's friend, Sabine. The pretty, fashionable neighbour who smiled and brought cakes. She was wearing trousers and a long coat, which was unusual because, to Anja, it seemed as if Sabine was dressed like a man. Something about that made Anja uncomfortable.

Without thinking, Anja turned her back and stared at the floor as if it would make her invisible.

When the red shoes reached the bottom of the stairs, they click-clacked across the hallway towards the exit, heels echoing on the patterned tiles.

Uncle Konrad had frozen with his hand still on the key, the key still in the lock.

Walk past. Walk past. Walk past, Anja repeated over and over in her head. *Walk past.*

But Sabine did not walk past. She stopped and faced the small group of escapees. Anja kept her eyes on the ground.

'Good evening, Herr Klein,' said Sabine with a soft voice. 'Frau Klein.'

Uncle finished locking the door then turned and nodded briefly. 'Good evening, Fräulein Engel.'

'Please,' she smiled. 'Call me Sabine.'

Aunt Trudi forced herself to return the smile then tried to usher Anja and Monika towards the building exit.

But Sabine moved to block the way.

'Out for a walk?' she asked.

Uncle cleared his throat. 'Yes, that's right.'

Anja kept her eyes down, watching those red shoes standing in front of her.

'But it's raining,' Sabine said.

'Not to worry,' said Uncle Konrad. 'We have our coats.'

'Yes,' Sabine replied. 'Yes, you do. I see that.'

Anja risked a glance up, lifting her head to see that the woman was looking right at her. *Staring*. Her icy blue eyes locked on to Anja's as if she could look into her mind and read her thoughts.

'You must be a friend of Monika's,' she said, holding out her hand for Anja to shake.

Anja wiped her sweaty palm on the front of her coat and took Sabine's hand. It was dry and soft. Her grip was tight.

'It's a pleasure to meet you.' Sabine looked Anja right in the eye and smiled.

She gave Anja the creeps. Her soft, oily voice. Her sly smile. Her tight handshake. The way her cold eyes bored right through her. Could she *really* be Monika's friend?

'We should go,' Uncle said.

'Yes, of course.' Sabine let go of Anja's hand. 'And so must I. I have somewhere important to be. Good evening.' She gave them another smile, then turned and headed across the hallway towards the exit.

That was when Anja noticed something that made her heart stop.

As Sabine stepped out into the rain, Anja noticed that she was holding a hat in her left hand. It was the kind of hat a man would wear.

Suddenly, Anja couldn't breathe.

A million thoughts and fears exploded inside her.

Uncle Konrad waited a moment, to be sure Sabine had left, then he led his band of escapees across the hallway towards the exit. But Anja had to force herself to move. It felt as if she were in a trance. As if she were in a bad dream, trying to run, but the ground had swallowed her feet.

Her breath came in small gasps as she followed the others out into the rain and down the steps on to the pavement. It was the first time Anja had been outside in days, but she couldn't appreciate the fresh air or enjoy the rain on her face. All she could think about was that woman. Sabine Engel.

The long raincoat. The hat in her hand.

Heading along the street, Anja dared to turn and watch Sabine walk away in the opposite direction. As she went, the woman moved to avoid the orange wash of light from the street lamps. She walked only in the shadow. And when she put on the hat and glanced back, Anja knew who she was.

6.58 p.m.

'It's her,' Anja said. They were halfway along the street when she finally found her voice. 'That's who I saw from my window.'

'What?' Aunt Trudi grabbed her hand. 'What do you mean?'

'When I was looking from my window and I thought someone was watching me? It was *her*. That woman. And she was there that night the soldiers shot the man in the alley. *She's* THE SHADOW.'

Anja looked at Monika, but Monika quickly glanced away.

'Are you sure?' asked Aunt Trudi.

'Yes. I recognize her hat.'

'Just keep walking,' said Uncle Konrad. 'Don't look back.'

Anja's mind was whirling like a spinning top. She thought about all the times she had seen THE SHADOW from her window. And she thought about something else too.

'Do you think it was her in the apartment?' Anja asked. 'Was it *her*? Do you think she's the one who came in when I had to hide in the wardrobe? Monika? Do you think it was her?'

'It couldn't be,' Monika said, still refusing to look Anja in the eye. 'Not her.'

'It doesn't matter now,' said Uncle Konrad. 'It's too late. Just keep walking.'

'But she's your friend,' Anja whispered to Monika. 'She's supposed to be your friend.'

Monika didn't reply.

7.01 p.m.

They stayed close together and tried not to attract attention. The streets were almost deserted, with just a few people passing by.

'If anyone stops us, don't say anything,' Uncle Konrad told them. 'Especially if it's the police. I'll do the talking. I'll say Anja is Monika's friend from school and we're taking her home; that's all.'

'What if they want to see identification?' Aunt Trudi asked. 'What if they ask questions?'

They all knew what she was thinking; it wouldn't take long for the police to find out that Anja didn't go to school with Monika and that she didn't live in East Berlin.

And that terrified Anja, because the police would call the Stasi. And the Stasi made people disappear.

'We'll be fine,' Uncle Konrad said. 'Just stay calm and we'll be fine.'

7.06 p.m.

'Walk a little faster now,' Uncle Konrad said as soon as they were away from the main streets. 'We don't have much time, and the train won't wait for us.'

But as they turned the corner, Anja caught sight of a dark shape on the rain-drenched pavement. It was low and close to the wall, moving in and out of the glimmering reflection of the street lamps on the puddles.

'Otto!' She couldn't help herself. She ran past Uncle Konrad, heading straight for her cat. He looked wet and miserable and meowed loudly when he recognized her.

For a moment, all her fears swept away. She was too excited and relieved to find Otto to think about anything else. But when she crouched to pick him up, he slipped past her outstretched hands and trotted on to the road.

'Otto! Come back!' Anja went after him.

'Leave him!' Uncle Konrad hissed. 'We're going to be late!'

But he was Anja's cat. Her friend. Her messenger. She couldn't just leave him. So, she chased Otto across the road until he stopped under the cover of a small tree and meowed loudly.

'Otto! Come here.' Anja went to take hold of him, but he moved again.

Uncle Konrad started across the street to stop her. Monika and Aunt Trudi stayed in the shadows on the other side.

'Anja,' Uncle Konrad said as he checked left and right. 'We don't have time.'

'Just one minute,' Anja insisted as she went after Otto, chasing him until she finally managed to get hold of him with both hands. He squirmed to get free, but Anja tucked him inside her coat and held him tight until he settled.

'Come along!' Uncle Konrad grabbed her arm harder than he needed to. 'They won't wait for us.'

7.12 p.m.

'What were you thinking?' Uncle Konrad said. 'Don't you know what will happen if we get caught?'

Aunt Trudi reached down to take Uncle's hand.

'We can't be late.' Uncle looked at his watch. 'I have timed it all very carefully, and Fräulein Engel has already delayed us. We have to be there by eight o'clock. The train won't wait for us.'

'I'm sorry,' Anja whispered.

7.43 p.m.

They walked as quickly as they dared, trying not to look afraid. Trying not to attract attention. They turned down one street after another, into parts of the city Anja had never visited before. They saw only a few people. A young couple sheltering beneath an umbrella as they hurried along the street. Two men standing on a dark corner who fell silent and looked down when the family passed by. A group of teenage boys who stopped laughing and watched them with suspicion.

And they stayed in the shadows as much as possible. On and on through the city.

Uncle Konrad led them far away, through a forest of tall grey buildings with a thousand windows glistening in the night, and into a scrubland dotted with leafless trees.

'Almost there.' Uncle Konrad's voice trembled. 'If we hurry, we might just make it.'

So, they ran. Now they thought they were away from spying eyes, they ran.

7.56 p.m.
Finally, they came to a chain-link fence topped with barbed wire that reminded Anja of the night this had all started. On the other side of the fence was a semicircle of dirty buildings, and beyond that were glimpses of the tangle of railway lines with engines and carriages waiting to be coupled together and sent out to carry passengers.

The train yard.

Uncle Konrad rushed to the fence and desperately began pushing at it with both hands. 'We don't have much time,' he said. 'There should be a gap. Jannick told me there would be a gap.' Uncle Konrad felt his way along the fence, becoming more and more frantic until—

'Yes! Here it is!' He found a section that had been cut. 'This is it!' He grabbed the wire with both hands and pulled it towards him. It took some effort before it was wide enough for them to crawl through.

'Quick!' Uncle Konrad held the flap of fence open for the others. 'Through here!'

Monika went first, then Anja, then Aunt Trudi. They got to their hands and knees and crawled through the wet dirt into the train yard.

Once they had all squeezed through, Uncle Konrad followed. 'All right,' he said. 'Come on. Hurry! We can still make it!'

Huddled close together, they hurried through the shadows. They crossed the tangle of rail tracks, darting among the idle engines and empty carriages. They slipped past grimy sheds and through patches where weeds sprouted from the ground.

But they were already too late.

8.01 p.m.

When they were almost halfway across the train yard, Anja heard voices and dogs barking. At first, the sound hardly registered because she was in such a hurry, but then Uncle Konrad stopped and said, 'Listen!'

They all came to a halt behind him.

Nobody said a word.

They stood together in the shadow of a dilapidated shed and listened to the growing commotion of barking and shouting.

Anja and the others exchanged worried glances, then followed Uncle Konrad as he edged forwards, creeping past the buildings and among the idle carriages and engines until they could see what was happening.

At the far end of the yard, beneath a huge metal roof, stood a single train of one engine and five carriages.

It was surrounded by police and soldiers.

Torches flickered backwards and forwards. Dogs strained at leads, barking as soldiers shouted and dragged women and children from the train, throwing them to the ground. Inside the carriages, silhouettes moved about in the dancing torchlight.

Anja and the others crouched in the shadows and watched, helpless.

'They found out,' Aunt Trudi whispered. 'The police found out about the escape.'

'But—' Uncle Konrad couldn't hide his distress. 'Someone must have told them. Who would—?'

'They have eyes and ears everywhere,' said Aunt Trudi. 'Informants. We're lucky we were late, otherwise we would have been on the train and . . . All we can do now is go home.'

'Go home?' Uncle Konrad replied. 'But what about Fräulein Engel? You saw the way she was looking at us. What if Anja is right about her being The Shadow? What if she's been spying on us and knows that Anja came through the tunnel and was in our apartment?'

'But . . . but even if she *is* The Shadow, how *could*

she know about Anja?' said Aunt Trudi. 'And how could she know about coming here? *How?*

Cold dread flowered in Anja's stomach as she thought back to when she had hidden in the wardrobe while someone searched the apartment. She was sure she had kept her journal with her both times but . . . what if she was wrong? What if she had left her journal out and someone – *Sabine* – had read it? What if the Stasi knew about the escape because Anja had written it in her journal?

The thought of it was too horrible. It would mean this was all her fault. All those people getting caught was *her* fault.

'I'm sure I had it with me,' Anja whispered to herself. 'I'm sure.'

But a sudden commotion of more barking tore Anja away from her thoughts. And this time, the sound was not coming from the train ahead of them.

It was coming from behind them.

8.06 p.m.

'They're surrounding us!' Monika started to panic as torchlight flickered among the disused carriages behind them. 'We have to surrender!'

'No,' Uncle Konrad said. 'We can't.'

'We have to,' Monika insisted. 'If we give up,

they'll let us . . . they *might* let us go. They might—'

'No way,' Uncle Konrad stopped her. 'Come on.'

They ran again, fast and silent. They kept in the shadows, ducking among the carriages and engines, staying ahead of the torches.

But the soldiers had dogs.

And the dogs had found the family's scent.

'What do we do?' Aunt Trudi asked when they stopped to catch their breath.

'I'm scared,' Monika moaned. 'We should surrender. Please.'

Anja said nothing. All she could think about was her journal burning a hole in her pocket. The journal that might have given them away. She cast her mind back, trying to remember if she'd had it with her in the wardrobe, or if she had left it out for someone to find. And in that moment, Anja hated her journal and she hated herself more than anything.

Otto squirmed inside her coat. He was uncomfortable, and the sound of the dogs was scaring him. Anja tried to calm him, but he dug his claws into her chest and wriggled free.

'Ow!'

He burst from the top of her coat and streaked across the train track towards a small and dirty concrete hut a few metres away from where they were hiding. Anja could just about make out the sign on the door:

Maintenance and Sewer Access: Keep Out.

A small section was missing from the bottom corner of the shabby door. Otto wriggled inside and disappeared.

When Anja started to go after him, Uncle Konrad stopped her. 'Leave him.'

Anja was about to protest, but had the sudden flash of an idea. A *clever* idea. Maybe even a brilliant one.

'Wait. What's in there?' Anja asked.

'It doesn't matter.' Aunt Trudi took a deep breath and looked back at the torches flashing in the night. 'They're getting closer; we have to keep moving.'

The sound of barking was growing louder by the second.

'It says "*sewer* access", Anja insisted. 'Is that tunnels?'

Uncle Konrad turned and looked at her. His eyes widened with realization, then he ran over to the concrete hut and pulled on the door handle.

'Damn,' he said. 'It's padlocked.'

8.10 p.m.
Monika stood by while Anja helped Uncle Konrad

and Aunt Trudi search for something they could use to smash the padlock.

'Come on, Monika,' Anja whispered to her. 'Help us! Do you *want* us to get caught?'

Monika glanced at Anja, then looked back at the torchlight flickering across the train yard as it headed towards them. She was rooted to the spot as if she was too scared to move.

'They're getting closer!' Aunt Trudi couldn't hide her fear. 'We have to go!'

'Wait!' Anja spotted a brick lying in a pile of rubble beside the maintenance hut. She darted over to grab it. 'Try this.'

Before she could even hold it up, Uncle Konrad snatched the brick from her hands and smashed the padlock with one strike.

He yanked open the door to reveal a small, dusty room. There was a dirt-covered table and chair in the far corner. An old, rusty wheelbarrow lay beside them, and an assortment of tools hung from racks on the walls.

Otto was sitting in the far corner, right on top of a cast-iron manhole cover. The compass round his neck glinted gently in the light that filtered in from the yard behind them.

Compasses are like magic, Helene had told Anja,

because they show you the way home.

'That's it!' Anja said with excitement as she pointed at the manhole cover. 'That's our way out. Right there.'

'It's too heavy,' Aunt Trudi replied. 'We'll never—'

'Try this.' Anja grabbed a crowbar from the rack on the wall and handed it to Uncle Konrad.

While Uncle Konrad wedged the crowbar under the manhole cover to prise it open, Aunt Trudi pulled Monika inside and shut the door to hide them from view. It was suddenly very dark in the maintenance hut, but just enough light leaked in through the cracks around the door for Aunt Trudi to snatch a shovel from the rack on the wall and wedge the blade of it under the door to keep it shut.

Anja went to Otto and scooped him into her arms.

'Clever boy,' she whispered as she tucked him back inside her coat. 'Clever boy.'

Uncle Konrad lifted the edge of the heavy manhole cover, then sat down and put his feet against it to push it out of the way. It squealed as it scraped across the concrete floor.

As soon as it was out of the way, Anja fished her torch from her pocket and shone it directly into the hole to reveal a ladder of metal rungs leading down into the darkness.

The sound of the dogs was almost on top of them now. Anja could hear the crunch of boots on the stones outside, and the harsh voices of the police shouting. She could hear the heavy panting of excited dogs.

'Get in.' Uncle Konrad beckoned Monika and helped her climb down.

8.18 p.m.
At the bottom of the ladder, Anja found herself on a stone walkway beside a river of sewage flowing into the darkness in front of her. The thick and dirty smell was overwhelming. It was even worse than it had been in the tunnel under her street. It felt like poison in her lungs.

Ahead, the tunnel was a never-ending blackness. Anja had images of being lost down there for ever, and her head began to spin, as it had done when she was squeezed into the hiding place in the wardrobe. A now familiar feeling of sickness swirled in her stomach and rose into her chest. The thought of heading into the darkness under the city filled her with dread, but the police and dogs chasing her were even more terrifying. There was no turning back now. Their only choice was to move forwards into the nightmare of the sewers.

They paused only long enough to make sure they were all down the ladder, then they ran, following the curve of the tunnel. The weak beam of Anja's torch bobbed up and down, glistening on the wet walls.

Anja counted her own footsteps. It was the best way for her to keep calm, but before long, lights flickered behind them and the sound of boots echoed in the cold, thick air.

'They're following!' Aunt Trudi panted.

'Keep running,' Uncle Konrad told them. 'Keep going.'

When they came to a split in the tunnel ahead, Uncle Konrad didn't hesitate to choose a direction. He took the right curve and continued into the blackness.

The further they ran, the more turns they took. First left, then right, then left again until they were lost in the maze of sewer tunnels beneath the city.

Anja's lungs burnt with the stink of sewage, and she longed to be free and above ground, but they saw no more ladders. No way to escape.

Eventually the sound of following footsteps faded, and Uncle Konrad stopped so they could catch their breath. For a while, the only sound was heavy breathing and the drip-drip-drip of water running down the dark and slimy walls.

Ahead, the tunnel split in three directions.

Three tunnels.

'Which one do we take?' Aunt Trudi asked.

Uncle Konrad took the torch from Anja and shone it into each tunnel before shaking his head.

'What if one of the tunnels takes us right back to where we started?' Monika asked. 'It feels like we've been going in circles. Should we surrender?'

'We'll be fine,' Uncle Konrad reassured her. 'We'll find a way out.'

'What if we don't?' There was a hint of panic in Monika's voice. 'What if we get stuck here for ever? If we surrender, they won't shoot us.'

Aunt Trudi wrapped her arms around Monika, and Anja felt a fresh surge of guilt.

This was her fault. *Her* fault.

'I'm sorry,' Anja said.

'It's not your fault,' said Uncle Konrad.

'No. It isn't,' Monika whispered.

'It is, though,' Anja sobbed. 'I'm the one who used the secret tunnel. I'm the one who got stuck on the wrong side of the wall. And . . . And I wrote about the escape plan in my journal. I don't think I left it out, but maybe I did. I mean, I must have done, and the person who broke into the apartment found it and read it and . . .' There. She had said it. Her guilty secret was out and it brought with it a flood of tears. 'It's all my fault.'

'You wrote it in your journal?' Uncle Konrad said through gritted teeth. 'Why would you write it in your journal? Why would you do that?'

'Stop it,' Aunt Trudi told him. 'You're scaring her. This isn't Anja's fault.' She turned to Anja. 'This isn't your fault. You didn't put the wall there. And if you hadn't stopped to get Otto, we wouldn't have been late for the train and we'd be caught already.'

Anja sniffed and looked at Monika, still in Aunt Trudi's arms. What Anja really wanted, more than anything, was for Monika to hug her and tell her it wasn't her fault. To tell her that they were still friends and would be friends for ever.

But Monika kept her eyes down, staring at the ground.

'You're right,' said Uncle Konrad. 'All that matters is finding a way out of here.' He flicked the torch from one tunnel to the other. Three tunnels. Three ways to run. But which was the right direction?

And then it came to her. The perfect idea.

'We want to go west,' Anja said.

'Yes.' Uncle Konrad sounded exhausted. 'But unless you know which way is—'

'I do.' Anja reached into her coat and felt for Otto's collar.

Otto squirmed to escape but Anja held him tight and flipped open the lid of the compass on his collar. Uncle Konrad shone his torch on the dial and they all peered at the needle as it swayed from side to side. Anja turned the compass so the needle was on N, just as Helene had shown her.

'So that tunnel must go west.' Anja pointed.

Uncle Konrad frowned. 'Good thinking. Come on.'

At that exact moment, lights flashed on the walls. A second later came the clack-clack of boot heels on concrete.

Anja held Otto tight in her coat as the shouts went up behind them.

'They're here!'

'This way!'

And then a storm of echoes surrounded the family. It sounded as if there were a hundred policemen behind them.

And they were close.

8.33 p.m.

Anja and the others ran as fast as they could, always going west. After a while, they sensed the tunnel begin to slope upwards. Anja's thighs burnt from the effort. Her lungs burnt from the stink of sewage. Her soul burnt with the guilt of having caused so much trouble. But she didn't stop.

She held Otto tight inside her coat and kept running.

In Uncle Konrad's hand, the torch beam jumped and flickered in the tunnel, picking out something metallic shining just ahead.

'A ladder!' he shouted. 'A way out. Hurry!'

Uncle Konrad didn't pause – he jumped on to the ladder and started climbing as soon as he reached it. His shoes clanged on the rungs.

'You next.' Aunt Trudi ushered Monika towards the ladder, encouraging her to step up on to the rungs.

The ladder wasn't long enough for anyone else, so Anja and Aunt Trudi waited on the tunnel floor, ready to climb.

When Uncle Konrad reached the top of the ladder, he pushed his shoulder against the manhole cover above him. It was heavy, but Uncle Konrad was strong. And desperate. He put all his strength into lifting that cover. His grunts of effort echoed around the tunnel, joining the clack-clack of approaching boots. And then the cover shifted. Just a few centimetres, but enough for Uncle Konrad to shove it aside with a squeal of metal on concrete.

Torchlight blinked close behind. Boot heels echoed. Louder and louder.

And when Anja turned, she saw police running towards her.

Two of them.

They would be here any moment.

'Go! Go!' Uncle Konrad shouted down as he climbed out. 'We're in the West. Quick!'

Monika began to scramble up the ladder. Anja was right behind her, just about to begin climbing, but Monika missed her footing and both feet slipped off the ladder. She hung on with both hands, swinging for a moment, kicking, frantically trying to get her feet back on the rungs.

'Help her!' Anja shouted to Aunt Trudi who clambered up the first few rungs and grabbed Monika's feet to direct them on to the ladder.

As soon as Monika was safe, she climbed quickly, Aunt Trudi following on her heels.

The police were closer. Anja could hear them breathing as she held Otto tight in her coat and grabbed a cold, slimy rung of the ladder.

'Stop!' someone shouted from behind. 'Stop!'

Anja didn't stop, but as soon as she was on the

ladder, she knew it would be impossible to climb one-handed. She had to let go of Otto. She was afraid that as soon as she did, the cat would slip from her coat, but instead, Otto gripped tight and clambered up towards Anja's shoulder. His claws pierced Anja's dress and scratched her skin, but she kept climbing. She reached for the next rung and looked up to see Aunt Trudi pull herself to freedom. Anja was almost there. Almost home. Just a few more rungs of the ladder and—

'Stop!'

The police were right behind her. She could *feel* them coming closer.

Monika's face appeared above, looking down in desperation. 'Quick!' she shouted. 'Hurry!'

But Anja was too slow. There came a sudden jolt as strong hands closed around her ankles and pulled her downwards. Anja dropped suddenly and her chin cracked against the ladder, sending pain firing through her jaw. For a second, she hung there, clinging on, with Otto squashed between her and the ladder, then the hands pulled again and she felt her fingers slipping from the rungs. She was going to fall. There was nothing she could do. She was caught.

'Anja!'

The last thing Anja heard was Monika scream-ing her name, then her grip tore away from the ladder and the police dragged her down into the darkness.

Ministry for State Security

Case Number 2372: Document I4.9.3

Letter written by Monika Klein, dated
7 October I96I.
Recovered from Anja Schumann after her
arrest on 7 October I96I.

7 October 1961

Dear Anja,

I am sitting here in my room while you are next door in the living room. I told you I have homework to do but really I wanted to write you this letter because I have so much to tell you even though I don't know what to say.

I have lied to you and betrayed you and I am the worst friend ever. I can't tell you what I have done until you are safe at home on the other side of the wall. So, I am going to write this and give you all my letters and then you will know all about the tunnel, the lies, Sabine, everything. But most of all you will know I betrayed you.

I hope you understand why I did it. I hope you

forgive me. You are my best friend in the whole world. I am so sad. Today is the last time I will see you but I still can't even look at you properly. I feel like my heart is broken.

I'm sorry.

I went to Sabine's apartment on Thursday night and told her everything. She kept meeting me after school and asking if I had found out anything, but there was never anything to tell, and she said Papa would get arrested for being a 'ringleader'. I have bruises on my arm from where she keeps grabbing me and pinching me. I'm so scared of her and what she will do. But then you told me that you're going home on Saturday, and that Papa has a plan, so I told Sabine. I had to. I sneaked up to her apartment in the night when you were asleep. She was scared that I was there and pulled me inside. She looked weird, as if her hair wasn't right, and I think she wears a wig. Everything about her is a lie. And her apartment is really bare. There were only two chairs and a small table in the living room, and I could see through to the kitchen and that looked really bare too. I don't know why, but all I could think was that there weren't even enough things in there for her to bake a cake like the one she gave me, so she must have lied about that too. Someone else must have made it, or she bought it. She didn't use her oma's recipe like she said.

I told her about the escape on Saturday but she just wanted to know what time and where and got really angry with me because I didn't know. She was trying not to shout and I thought she was going to hurt me. I started to get really scared that I shouldn't have gone to her apartment. Then I remembered your journal and I said maybe you had written something in there. She said she would use her key to come into the apartment and read it herself, and that's what she did. I know that because you had to hide again and because Sabine was waiting for me at the subway station after school and she told me. But she didn't find your diary so you must have had it with you. She told me I had to read it and that if I didn't, she would arrest Mama and Papa!

When I got back from school, you were shaking and scared because you'd had to hide in the wardrobe again and stay there for ages. I felt so horrible because it was my fault and I sat with you and talked to you but I couldn't even look at you without feeling guilty. When Mama and Papa got back from work, and you were telling them what happened, I came into my bedroom and took your journal from under the mattress. I looked at some of what you'd written and it made me feel so mean and horrible. It's bad to read someone's journal, especially if they are your best friend. But at least I found out something that might keep everyone safe. I found out that the escape is at the train yard on Saturday at eight o'clock, so when everyone was asleep, I went upstairs to tell Sabine, but I wouldn't tell her until she'd promised to let you go, and to not arrest Mama and Papa. So, she promised and I told her everything. She said I mustn't say anything and that Papa must take you to the train yard exactly as planned. When the police arrest everyone, they will take you home, and Papa will be allowed to come home too. She said they will have to arrest Papa first, but then they will bring him home. She said I'm a 'true hero of the German Democratic Republic', but I don't feel like a hero. I feel like a traitor. Someone already got shot because of me, and I have lied to Mama and Papa and to you. I have betrayed you all and I have even read your journal which is the worst thing a friend can do.

But you are going to be safe. Sabine has promised.

I hope Mama and Papa will forgive me. I hope *you* will forgive me. I am going to write a note for the compass and I will hide all my letters and notes inside your journal so when you get home tonight you can find them and read them. Then you will know what I have done.

Please forgive me.

Your best friend,
Monika

SATURDAY 7 OCTOBER 1961

<u>8.44 p.m.</u>
For Monika, the next moments passed in a dream-like daze.

She watched in horror as her best friend's hands ripped free from the ladder.

Anja's chin hit the rung in front of her, hard enough for Monika to hear the clang as the metal vibrated. Her head snapped backwards, her eyes rolled up in her head, then she dropped into the tunnel and landed with a hard thump on the stones below. Illuminated by the soldiers' torches, she lay in a crumpled heap, not moving.

She was dead.

Monika was sure of it.

The soldiers had dragged Anja down and they had killed her as surely as they had killed the man who was shot trying to swim across the canal. As surely as they had killed the man in the alley close to her apartment.

Soldiers surrounded Anja's body, dropping to their knees beside her as Otto crawled, confused, from the folds of her coat. Within seconds, the tunnel was filled with noise and confusion. More men and women in uniform came into view, all of them with guns. Some of them held on to dogs straining at leads, growling and snarling, excited even more by the presence of a cat.

It was as if every soldier in East Berlin was crammed into the sewers.

In the bedlam of noise and confusion, Monika saw Otto scurry towards the ladder and press himself tight against the wall. He was trapped. There was no way for him to escape.

Then one of the soldiers looked up and saw Monika peering down.

Immediately, he lifted his rifle and aimed at her.

'Get back here!' he yelled. 'Surrender!'

Other soldiers began to raise their rifles, but before Monika could respond, she felt arms grab her tight around the waist and lift her off the ground.

'We have to go,' Papa said, turning Monika around and carrying her away from the manhole. 'We have to get away from here right now.'

'No!' Monika struggled out of his grasp. 'No!' She scrambled back to the manhole and dropped to her knees to look down. More soldiers were pointing their weapons up at her, but Monika wasn't looking at them. She didn't care about them. She was looking at Anja, still lying in a terrible, awful, horrible heap at the bottom of the ladder. She hadn't moved. Not an inch.

Raw pain welled inside Monika's body. It boiled in her veins and burnt in her stomach. It rose like hot lava.

'Anja!' she screamed.

And then Papa grabbed her again, pulling her away.

It was the last time Monika ever saw Anja.

<u>8.47 p.m.</u>

'We have to run,' Papa said. 'There's nothing we can do for Anja.'

They were in a dark alley, surrounded by rubbish and high brick walls. Papa was holding tight to Monika's arm, dragging her towards the place where the alley opened on to a well-lit street.

Mama hurried alongside them, saying, 'I'm so sorry. I'm so sorry,' over and over, trying to comfort her.

'I can't leave her,' Monika shouted. 'I can't leave her.' The words clawed at her throat, but it was as if Mama and Papa couldn't hear her. The world was closing in as if she was back in the dark room from her nightmare. She felt as if she were being crushed, and it was all her fault.

Anja was dead and it was all. Her. Fault.

The pain and horror of it was too much to bear. She struggled to break free from Papa, but he put both arms around her and lifted her off her feet. He held her tight and pressed his face against hers as he carried her along the alley.

'If we go back, they'll arrest us.' Papa spoke quietly. 'I'm so sorry.'

'But she's dead!' Monika screamed as she kicked out, trying to escape. 'She's dead and it's all my fault. We have to go back.'

'It's *not* your fault.' Papa held firm. 'None of this is your fault.'

'But it is!' Monika sobbed. 'It's *all* my fault. I told them about the escape. I read Anja's journal. I'm a horrible person and it's all my fault.'

With those words, Monika's strength left her. It was as if she were a light that had been suddenly switched off. Her body sagged, and before Papa could stop her, she slipped through his arms and collapsed to the ground.

'She promised,' Monika said. 'She promised.'

'What are you talking about?' Papa reached down to pull her up. 'Who promised?'

'Sabine,' Monika said, hanging her head. 'Sabine promised.' She was exhausted now. She had no more energy left.

'Oh, Monika,' Mama said, crouching beside her. 'What did you do?'

But Monika didn't have the chance to tell her, not until much later, because two soldiers emerged from the shadows with their rifles raised. Otto was there, coiling around their legs as if everything were normal.

'Come back now,' one of the soldiers ordered. 'Or we'll shoot.'

Papa turned around to face them. 'You won't shoot,' he said. 'Not here. Not in the West.'

'Do you really want to find out?' the soldier replied.

Papa's shoulders slumped. He looked at Monika, still on her knees, then at Mama crouching beside her.

'Almost,' he whispered. 'We almost made it.'

When they walked back towards the soldiers,

Otto meowed loudly, trotted deeper into the alley, and disappeared into the shadows.

<u>8.59 p.m.</u>
When Monika reached the bottom of the ladder, Anja was gone. All that remained of her was a dark stain of blood on the stone floor of the sewer.

Monika was numb. Too empty to cry. Too distressed to know where she was. She could hardly even remember to breathe as the soldiers ushered her forward to make room for Mama and Papa coming down the ladder.

All she could do was stare at that dark patch of blood glistening on the dirty stones.

It was all that was left of Anja.

<u>9.03 p.m.</u>
As soon as Mama and Papa were back inside the sewer tunnel, soldiers came forward and cuffed their wrists as if they were criminals. They did the same to Monika, making her wince at the metallic click and snap as the cuffs tightened around her bony wrists. And when Monika looked down at her hands, she saw blood on them and she knew it was Anja's. It must have been on the rungs of the ladder, from when Anja had banged her chin. From when the

soldiers had dragged her down.

'Move!' one of the soldiers ordered, and the family began their long walk back.

Monika put one foot in front of the other and followed, but she held her hands out in front of her and stared at them. She could not take her eyes off the blood as it dried on her skin. It was as if something had broken inside her. She could think of nothing. She couldn't cry. All she could do was look at that blood in the torchlight as she trudged through the maze of tunnels.

Finally, after an eternity underground, they climbed back up into the maintenance hut and emerged into the train yard. The soldiers immediately ordered the family onwards, picking through the abandoned carriages and piles of junk, to the place where the lights were blazing.

'Halt!' one of the soldiers eventually shouted.

Monika and her parents came to a stop beside a pile of rusted metal and twisted wire. They were still several metres away from the captured train, but Monika could see what was happening ahead. She could see the full extent of her betrayal; the result of the information she had given to Sabine Engel.

The train stood idle on the tracks, exposed by the harsh glow of electric lights. A single engine, coupled to a line of five carriages. All the carriage doors were open now, and the lights were on inside. Behind the windows, the shadowy shapes of soldiers moved along the aisles, leading dogs that checked and rechecked every seat and every dark corner. More soldiers patrolled outside, flashing torches as they searched the rest of the train yard.

Behind the last carriage, a line of prisoners knelt on the sharp stones beside the track. At least twenty people – men, women and children.

Standing in front of them, flanked by soldiers, were a man and a woman dressed in the uniforms of Stasi officers. As Monika watched, the Stasi officers ordered the prisoners to their feet and soldiers began loading them into the back of grey vans that were waiting with their engines running.

One of the soldiers who had brought Monika and her parents from the sewers jogged over towards the Stasi officers. When the female Stasi officer noticed him coming towards her, she walked out to meet him. With the bright lights behind her she was a tall silhouette, with broad shoulders in her uniform jacket. She walked upright, with the confidence of someone who is in charge.

She stopped as the soldier reached her, halfway between Monika's group and the captured train. She was close enough for Monika to see that her face was pale and she had blonde hair pulled back in a harsh ponytail.

The Stasi officer and the soldier spoke for a while before they broke apart and the soldier returned to where Monika and her parents were standing. He stopped in front of Monika and looked down at her.

'Come with me,' he said.

'What?' Papa protested. 'No. You can't. She's just a child.' He tried to step forward, but one of the other soldiers held him back.

The soldier who had spoken to the Stasi officer glared at Papa, then reached out and grabbed Monika's cuffed hands. 'Come with me,' he repeated as he dragged Monika away.

He took her past the place where the prisoners were being loaded into vans and towards a shiny black car parked beyond them.

'Get in,' he ordered as he opened the back door and pushed Monika inside.

The Stasi officer with the blonde ponytail was already sitting in the passenger seat, facing forwards. The soldier went around to the driver's side, climbed in and started the engine.

No one spoke as the car pulled out of the train yard.

Monika felt empty as the black car drove deeper into the heart of the city. They passed among the crowds of buildings with lights twinkling in their windows. All she could do was stare at her hands. And every time they drove beneath street lights, or passed another vehicle, the inside of the car lit up and Monika saw the stain on her fingers, black like tar. Then the lights passed and the inside of the car was dark again and the stain faded from view. But Monika knew it was there. It would *always* be there, because there was no way for her to right all her wrongs. No way for her to turn back time. All she could do now was accept what was happening to her. She didn't even care any more. She wanted to disappear and to have never been born, because she would never be able to forgive herself for what she had done.

After a long time or a short time, Monika didn't know which, the black car stopped at a barrier. They waited for it to lift before driving along a narrow alleyway to a small courtyard concealed behind a large grey building. When the car stopped, the woman with the ponytail spoke quietly to the driver, who climbed out and opened the back door.

'With me,' he said to Monika.

Monika didn't respond, so the soldier leant in to take hold of her and encourage her out of the vehicle. He kept hold of her arm as he led her across the dark courtyard towards a black door. Beside the door was a large metal box with a single button and a speaker. The soldier pressed the button and, somewhere behind the door, a buzzer sounded.

A few moments later, a voice crackled through the speaker.

'Identification.'

The soldier leant close and mumbled into the speaker, then came a long buzz followed by a click.

The soldier pushed open the door and shoved Monika into a long, brightly lit corridor lined with more doors, each with a large white number painted on it.

The soldier took Monika to the far end of the corridor and opened the door marked Number 1. Behind door Number 1 was a small, grey-walled room that smelt of sweat and fear. To one side, a metal table was bolted to the wall. A chair was fixed to the floor on either side of it. The only other thing in the room was a reel-to-reel recording device attached to the wall by the table.

The soldier ushered Monika into the room, then closed the door behind her and bolted it shut.

Monika stood alone in the centre of the grey room.

It was dim in there. The only light was from a single bare bulb that hung from a wire directly above the metal table. There were no windows, just grey walls and a grey floor.

Somewhere in the building voices were shouting. Someone was screaming.

But Monika hardly noticed any of it. All she could do was stare at her hands.

Anja's blood.

The thought went around and around inside her head, pushing everything else out.

Anja's blood.

Footsteps sounded in the corridor outside. Firm and quick. It was the sound of hard heels on a hard floor.

The footsteps came closer and closer. Louder and louder.

They came right to the door marked Number 1, and then they stopped.

There was a moment of silence, as if the world was holding its breath, then came the metallic scrape of a bolt being drawn back, and the door swung open.

The Stasi officer standing in the doorway was the same one Monika had seen at the train yard. The same one who had travelled in the car with her.

She was tall and broad-shouldered. Her skin was pale and without make-up. Her blonde hair was pulled back tight into a ponytail.

'Monika,' the officer said. 'Why don't you sit down?'

The officer came forward and took Monika's arm. But not firmly, the way the male soldier had gripped her. The officer was gentle. Her touch was considerate.

'Come on,' she said as she led Monika to one of the metal chairs and helped her sit down. 'Let me take these off.' She placed a large brown envelope on the tabletop, then took a small key from her pocket. She unlocked Monika's handcuffs and slipped the cold metal from her wrists.

The officer tucked the handcuffs into her pocket and went to the other side of the table. She eased herself into the chair opposite Monika.

'Anja is on her way home,' the officer said. 'As promised.'

The words were like a bolt of lightning.

'Anja's alive?' Monika looked up sharply. 'She's alive?'

'Yes,' the woman replied. 'She's a little bruised, but she's alive. She'll be crossing the border as we speak.'

With those words, relief flooded into Monika.

Her whole body came back to life and her chest hitched as she gasped for breath between great sobs. Tears welled in her eyes and poured down her cheeks.

But somewhere beneath her relief, there came a sudden recognition.

Now that Monika looked at the officer – *really* looked at her – she realized she knew who she was.

She was Sabine.

The Stasi officer was Sabine.

Sabine reached over to the recording device and switched it on.

Ministry for State Security

File Number 2372

Transcript of interview between Captain
█████████ (code name: Sabine Engel) and
Monika Klein, Saturday 7 October I96I.

MONIKA KLEIN:	It's you. You're Sabine.
CAPTAIN ████████ :	For the recording, the date is 7 October 1961. The time is thirty-five minutes past ten. I am Captain ████████ , known throughout this operation as 'Sabine Engel', and the interview is with Monika Klein. Monika, please state your date of birth.
MONIKA KLEIN:	Sabine isn't even your real name.
CAPTAIN ████████ :	Monika, please state your date of birth.
MONIKA KLEIN:	Anja is alive?
CAPTAIN ████████ :	Your date of birth, Monika.
MONIKA KLEIN:	Anja is alive?
CAPTAIN ████████ :	For the recording, Monika Klein's date of birth is 26 April 1949. Yes, Monika, it's me. And yes, Anja is alive. She is a little bruised, and she has a cut on her chin, but she has been treated and she is being taken to the border. Western authorities will meet her there and take her home.

MONIKA KLEIN:	She's alive.
CAPTAIN ▮▮▮▮▮:	Yes. And your parents will soon be home also. They will be processed with everyone else who was arrested at the train yard, but they will be taken home once that is done. We have to keep up appearances, you understand. If we simply let them go, people will be suspicious. And you, of course, will be free to go as soon as this interview is finished.
MONIKA KLEIN:	I hate you.
CAPTAIN ▮▮▮▮▮:	You've done excellent work, Monika. Your information has led to the arrest of twenty-seven traitors to our country. We have identified and arrested the organizers of a huge escape plot. You should be proud of yourself. You are a hero of the German Democratic Republic.
MONIKA KLEIN:	You made me betray everyone.

CAPTAIN ▮▮▮▮▮▮▮▮: You're a hero, Monika. You showed great bravery and dedication to your country. Perhaps one day you might come and work for us. You might even work for me.

MONIKA KLEIN: I'd rather die.

CAPTAIN ▮▮▮▮▮▮▮▮: I'm sorry to hear you say that. But perhaps you will change your mind in time. I have fulfilled every part of our agreement. I have been nothing but fair.

MONIKA KLEIN: I thought you were my friend. You tricked me.

CAPTAIN ▮▮▮▮▮▮▮▮: Anja had these in her coat pocket. For the benefit of the recording, I am taking a journal and a bundle of letters and notes from a large brown envelope. The journal was written by Anja Schumann, and the letters are yours, Monika. Letters that you wrote to Anja during the past months. I haven't had time to read them in detail, but I have looked through them and I can see that you never sent them to

Anja. She hasn't read them, and I'm afraid she never will. They will be kept in your file here at headquarters, along with Anja's journal and the notes you passed to each other.

MONIKA KLEIN: She'll never know it was my fault. That you tricked me.

CAPTAIN ███████: No. But she will be home with her family. And you will be home with yours. Where you both belong.

MONIKA KLEIN: I hate you so much.

CAPTAIN ███████: The purpose of this interview, Monika, is to officially thank you for the work you have done in leading to the uncovering of a fascist plot against our great country. You may not divulge any details of this case to anyone at any time. If we find that you have divulged any information, you and your family will be arrested. And please be sure of this . . . we will be watching you. Always.

Interview ends.

SATURDAY 7 OCTOBER 1961

<u>Sometime after 10 p.m.</u>
Monika watched through tears as Sabine gathered the journal, and her letters to Anja, and slipped them back into the brown envelope.

Sabine put the envelope on the table in front of her and stared at it. She paused, then took a deep breath and looked up at Monika.

'For what it's worth, Monika, I'm sorry. For everything that has happened to you. Sometimes we have no choice. Sometimes . . . sometimes we are forced to do things we don't want to do. To protect the people we love. I know you can understand that.'

Sabine closed her eyes for a long time, and when

she opened them again, they glistened in the dim glow from the single light bulb above the table. She sniffed once, then stood up and wiped both eyes with her fingers. She picked up the brown envelope that contained the letters Anja would never read.

'I'm sorry, Monika,' she said. 'For all of it. I never wanted to hurt you.'

Sabine turned around and went to the door. She banged once and there came the sound of the bolt being drawn back.

When the door opened, Sabine spoke to the soldier who opened it.

'You can take her home now,' she said. 'We're done.'

Ministry for State Security

File Number 2372

Case Summary:

Konrad Klein was given employment at Becker
Steel, working in a department with men
suspected of aiding the escape of several
citizens. Given Konrad Klein's connections
to the West, it was predicted that he would
soon make contact with the plotters. Captain
████████ (code name: Sabine Engel) was
placed in Apartment 4, No. 2I Gartenstrasse
to watch Konrad Klein, and gather
information leading to the arrest of the
plotters. Captain ████ did an exemplary job,
seizing an opportunity to gain the
confidence of Monika Klein, daughter of
Konrad and Trudi Klein. This relationship
allowed Captain ████ to gather important
information leading to the arrest of twenty-

seven traitors to the GDR on Saturday 7
October I96I.

The building where the Klein family lived
was demolished on II October I96I. The
family was relocated to a new apartment on
Bahnhofstrasse. The Klein family is not
permitted to leave the GDR at any time, and
remains under surveillance.

Anja Schumann was taken to the border at
Friedrichstrasse and transferred into the
hands of Western authorities.

All charges against ███████████, the
husband of Captain ██████████ (code name:
Sabine Engel), were dropped as reward for
Captain ██████ display of loyalty to the
GDR. Captain ██████ and her husband remain
under surveillance.

Case Closed.

Update: Information suggests that the
Schumann family made several unsuccessful
attempts to trace the whereabouts of the
Klein family. They finally left West Berlin
on I5 December I962 to take up residence in
England, United Kingdom.

RETURN
NOVEMBER 1989

COMMUNISTS OPEN BERLIN WALL AND BORDERS TO THE WEST

Yesterday Communist East Germany took the momentous decision to open its borders to the West. Checkpoints in the Berlin Wall were opened for citizens to travel freely.

As word spread across the city, excited East Berliners flooded to the borders and poured into West Berlin. For some, it was their first journey into the western half of the city, which has been divided by a thirteen-foot wall for twenty-eight years.

On the western side, huge crowds gathered, bringing bottles of champagne and passing them around. Fireworks erupted over the city, and street festivals went on into the early hours of the morning.

Close to the Brandenburg Gate, scores of young West and East Germans climbed the wall to greet each other; singing, shouting and waving flags. Some brought hammers and chisels – using them to break off parts of the wall, which is the most visible sign of the 'Iron Curtain' – the division between eastern and western Europe.

Instead of tense confrontations between American and Soviet troops, last night there was a sense of joy. Instead of life-or-death scenes of East Germans trying to cross the heavily fortified border, there was celebration.

Most of all, there was hope. Hope for a future without division.

10 NOVEMBER 1989

Anja reread the article twice as the plane bumped down on to the runway, then she folded the newspaper on to her lap and stared out of the small round window.

She watched the airport come into view as the plane coasted towards the terminal building.

The pilot's voice was crackling over the speakers. He was saying something about the time and the temperature and that he hoped everyone had had a pleasant flight. But Anja wasn't listening.

Anja was thinking about the wall and the compass. She was thinking about Otto the cat, a lost best friend and a stolen journal. She was thinking about Monika, a friend she hadn't seen or heard from since that dreadful night in the dark sewers, twenty-eight years ago. And she was remembering how it had all been her fault. If she hadn't sneaked through the tunnel under the wall, if she hadn't left her journal out for the intruder to read, if she hadn't been such a silly girl, everything would be different.

Anja lifted a hand to touch the scar on her chin and, for a moment, she was right back there in the darkness, trying to cling to the cold and slimy rungs of the ladder. She had tried to hold on. She had tried so hard to get away, but it had been impossible once the soldier grabbed her. And when she hit her chin, everything went dark. What came after that was mostly a blur. Soldiers carried her back through the tunnels. They took her to the border and through the checkpoint to a waiting police car.

Within a few hours, she was at home in bed, with Mama and Papa by her bedside, relieved to have her home. But it was a long time before Anja felt any relief.

Now, sitting in the plane as it finally came to a stop, Anja felt the shadow of the nightmares that had plagued her since the night she returned home. Even as an adult, the nightmares still came.

Sometimes Anja dreamt she was buried alive, lying paralysed beneath the soil. Other times, terrible monsters in Stasi uniforms chased her through narrow sewers with soft floors that sucked at her feet. But most of all Anja dreamt about Monika. She dreamt that her best friend was chained to the wall in some cold, damp dungeon. She was forgotten there, left alone and afraid. And it was all Anja's fault.

Even now, at the age of forty, Anja still sometimes woke with tears on her pillow.

A few days after Anja came home, bulldozers knocked down the buildings on the other side of the wall, and just like that, Monika's apartment was nothing but dust. And when Mama and Papa tried to find out what had happened to Monika and the rest of the family, it was like staring into a black hole. There was no trace of them.

The wall grew higher and wider. The East German authorities built towers and minefields. They dug trenches and positioned machine guns and put down beds of nails.

Eventually Mama and Papa decided it was best to leave Berlin. It was the only way to make Anja's nightmares go away.

But they never did go away. Not completely.

And now it was twenty-seven years since Anja had set foot in Berlin.

*

Anja left the plane and entered the airport building with a strange sense of hope and dread. She felt the excitement in the air around her. There was a buzz she had never felt before.

'Can you believe it?' someone was saying in the queue behind her. 'They've opened the borders. They just . . . they're just letting people through.'

'I'm going to see my sister,' said a man with grey hair and tears in his eyes.

He carried a newspaper which screamed the headline: 'WE ARE ONE NATION!'

And when Anja emerged from the airport to wait for a taxi, it was as if the air in Berlin was charged with electricity. Her skin prickled and her hair stood on end. Her heart beat harder now that she was here, closer to where it had all happened. She began to wonder if she would be able to make it all the way to her old apartment without her heart bursting right out of her chest.

Her taxi driver was a big man with ruddy cheeks and an impressive moustache that turned up at the ends.

'Where to?' he asked with a smile when Anja climbed in, so she told him the address. It felt odd speaking to a stranger in German instead of English. For years, she had spoken German only with her parents.

'Streets are busy,' the taxi driver said as he pulled away from the terminal building and into the line of traffic. 'Have you come to see someone?'

Anja looked out of the window. 'See someone?' she asked.

'Someone you haven't seen for a long time, I mean? I've had lots of passengers coming to see friends. Brothers. Sisters. Mamas and papas. Everyone lost someone when the wall went up, you know. Everyone. But now we can come and go as we please. Thousands of Easterners have come through. How about you? You lose someone?'

'Yes.' Anja touched the scar on her chin. 'I lost Monika. My best friend in all the world.'

'How old were you?'

'Twelve and three quarters,' Anja replied.

'Very specific,' the taxi driver said. 'It must have been hard.'

'It was. But I don't think I'll ever see her again.'

'You never know,' the driver shrugged. 'Miracles happen.'

Anja forced herself to smile. 'I don't think so. No. All I want to do is stand on the steps of my old apartment and look at the wall and know it's over. It's finished.'

And then the nightmares might stop, she thought.

The taxi driver nodded. 'I can understand that.'

The journey through the heavy traffic was slow, and as they drove deeper into the city, Anja began to see crowds of people in the streets. Young and old moving towards the wall. Further still, and the roads were so crammed that the taxi finally came to a stop, hemmed in on all sides by cars and crowds of people. The air was filled with excited chatter and honking horns.

'We're close enough,' Anja told the taxi driver. 'I'll get out here.'

'I'm not sure we'll get much closer anyway!' The taxi driver laughed and hooted his horn three times. All around, an orchestra of car horns joined him. Someone passed by the front of the taxi, waving at the driver and dancing for a moment before heading on to do the same to the car in front.

'Thank you.' Anja paid the driver and stepped out into the tidal wave of celebration. It almost swept her away.

She moved among the cars to the side of the road as a tight feeling gathered in her chest and welled into her throat. It was as if hidden emotions were forcing themselves out from somewhere deep inside her. Anja took a deep breath and pushed the feelings away. She glanced around to get her bearings. Things had changed, but she knew where she was. She had been on these streets a thousand times when she was twelve years old.

And now she was that age again. Twelve years old, and on her way home from the park.

She followed the crowds until the wall was in sight, then she turned and headed along Gartenstrasse towards home. She didn't see the thousands of people surging around her. She hardly even glanced at the young men and women standing on top of the wall, waving flags and singing. She took no notice of those who struck the wall with sledgehammers and pickaxes. Even when revellers grabbed her and tried to dance with her, or hand her bottles of champagne to drink from, Anja just smiled and brushed them off. Instead, she focused on moving forwards, pushing through the crowd and following the street towards her old apartment.

She was twelve years old again. A little girl with her whole life ahead of her.

She was twelve years old, and she was going home.

On the other side of the wall, where Monika's apartment building had once stood, there was nothing but sky. But Anja's old building was still there, and the steps were still there. The same steps from which she had waved to Monika across the barbed wire. The same steps she had stood upon to watch the wall grow higher and higher.

People were crowded on to those steps, dancing and jumping up and down. They were shouting words of encouragement to a group of boys who were smashing at the wall with crowbars, chipping away at the concrete.

But one person on the steps was standing completely still.

A woman. Slim, and small, with short dark hair.

And she was staring directly at Anja.

Anja knew instantly who she was, and her emotions rose like a tidal wave. The sound of the crowd disappeared. Her chest tightened so she could hardly breathe. Tears welled in her eyes, and her legs weakened.

She couldn't move as the woman came down the steps and through the crowd towards her.

Anja couldn't take her eyes off the woman. It was as if there was no one else in the world. But to Anja's eyes, she wasn't a woman at all; she was a dark-haired girl, and the best friend anyone could ever have.

And when the dark-haired girl was standing in front of Anja, they were both twelve years old again.

'Hello,' said Monika.

Anja couldn't speak. Her throat was too tight. Her

tears were too strong. Instead, she reached up and took a gold chain from around her neck. Hanging at the end of the chain was a small compass.

'Otto found his way home,' Anja eventually managed to say.

'Clever Otto,' Monika smiled.

'Clever Otto,' Anja repeated. 'But the compass should always go forwards. Never backwards. That's what Helene told me. I think I understand what that means now. It means the compass is yours.'

With trembling fingers, Monika took the compass and opened it to see a tiny piece of paper wedged inside the lid. She stared at it as if she couldn't believe it was still there.

'Is that . . .?' Monika whispered. 'Is that . . .?'

'Yes,' Anja said. 'The last message you ever sent. I kept it there this whole time.'

Gently, Anja took the scrap of paper from the lid of the compass and unfolded it to reveal the faded message Monika had written all those years ago.

Please forgive me. Love M.

'I have so much to tell you,' Monika said, looking up at her friend. 'Can you ever forgive me?'

'Yes,' Anja said. 'Whatever you did, I forgive you. Can *you* forgive *me*?'

'There's nothing to forgive.' Monika sobbed and put her arms around Anja. 'Nothing at all.'

They stood like that for a long time, holding on as if they would never let go.

GLOSSARY

checkpoint   Official crossing place in the Berlin Wall.

Die Farbenelf   A popular German card game for one player.

Frau   Conventional German term of address for a married woman (Mrs).

Fräulein   Conventional German term of address for an unmarried woman (Miss).

FRG   Federal Republic of Germany, also known as West Germany.

GDR   German Democratic Republic, also known as East Germany.

Herr   Mr.

informant   A person who gives information about their friends and neighbours to the authorities.

mark(s)   The official currency of East Germany.

schnitzel   A thin slice of meat that is breaded and fried.

Stasi   The East German secret police organization. One of the most feared and hated institutions of East Germany, it was officially known as the Ministry for State Security and was responsible for surveillance and espionage.

Volkspolizei The national police force of East Germany.

Young Pioneers A youth organization for children aged 6–13.

DID YOU KNOW?

In 1945, at the end of World War II, Germany was divided into four zones. The zones were controlled by four different countries: the United Kingdom, France, the United States and the Soviet Union. Berlin, the capital of Germany, was also divided into four zones.

In 1949, the UK, France and USA zones became West Germany (and West Berlin), and the Soviet Union zone became East Germany (and East Berlin). They were two different countries, with different governments and different ways of life. Although people were restricted from travelling between East and West Germany, things were different in the capital city. Berliners were able to cross from East Berlin to West Berlin whenever they wanted. Millions of East German people used this as a way to leave East Germany, where life was hard and the government was cruel.

At midnight on 13 August 1961, East German authorities built a barrier of barbed wire and cinder blocks along the border to stop their citizens from leaving. Soon after, they began construction of the Berlin Wall which surrounded West Berlin, turning it into an island in the middle of East Germany.

When the Berlin Wall was finally completed, it was actually two walls. The sandy area between the walls was known as the 'Death Strip', and was guarded by towers, spikes, electrified fences, landmines, dogs and machine guns.

The Berlin Wall was approximately 155 kilometres long, and was five metres high in some places.

There were only three official places to cross the Berlin Wall. These were called checkpoints. The most famous checkpoint was in the centre of Berlin at Friedrichstrasse and was known to the US and UK military as 'Checkpoint Charlie'.

It is estimated that before it was finally brought down, 5,000 people escaped into West Berlin by going over, under or through the Berlin Wall. One of the very first people to escape was an East German soldier called Konrad Schumann who jumped over the barbed wire on 15 August 1961. Other escapes were made at different times using different methods such as zip wire, tightrope, hot air balloon, bulldozer, tank and even a model cow.

On 5 December 1961, an engine driver named Harry Dieterling used a passenger train to help thirty-two of his friends and family escape from East Berlin. They lay on the floor of the carriage as he crashed the train through the Berlin Wall. No one was injured, but seven passengers and the train conductor, who knew nothing about the escape plan, immediately walked back to East Berlin.

Not all escape attempts were successful. Approximately 200 people were killed trying to escape from East Berlin to West Berlin.

At midnight on 9 November 1989, restrictions were ended and people were finally free to pass through the Berlin Wall.

ACKNOWLEDGEMENTS

My thanks go to all the brilliant people at Chicken House who bring my books to life – Barry, Esther, Liv, Laura, Jazz, Elinor, Emily and especially Rachel L who helped me find the heart of this story and supported me when I tried to do something a little different. Rachel L's cheery encouragement during our long chats always leaves me feeling uplifted. Thanks to Claire whose incredible eye for detail was vital to unravelling a complicated timeline, to Rachel H and Matthew for the beautiful cover illustration, and of course to my agent, Ella, who always has my back. Thanks to you, awesome reader, for your never-ending awesomeness, and to all the librarians, book-sellers, bloggers and story lovers who spread the word! Oh, and a great big 'cheers' to the DKW Thursday Therapy gang. Most of all, though, thanks to my wife and my children for all the brightness they bring – I couldn't do it without them.

NISHA'S WAR

1942

Nisha has escaped the terror of the Japanese invasion of Singapore. Missing the heat of home in Malaya, her grandmother's house in the North of England seems especially cold and grey. Even the villagers are suspicious of a girl with brown skin who they can see is only half English. One night, a boy beckons to Nisha from the treehouse she is forbidden to play in. Or at least, she thinks he's a boy. And for lonely Nisha, the chance of finding a friend is worth almost anything.

What a story! Absolutely gripping! Touches of The Secret Garden and The Woman in Black. Bravo Dan Smith, I loved it!
EMMA CARROLL

Paperback, ISBN 978-1-912626-75-5, £7.99 • ebook, ISBN 978-1-913696-16-0, £7.99